LLOYD JONES

Lloyd Jones is the author of ten novels and collections of stories. *Here at the end of the world we learn to dance* was shortlisted for the Deutz Medal for Fiction at the 2002 Montana Book Awards. *The Book of Fame* won the Deutz Medal a year later.

The first of his novels to be published in the UK, *Mister Pip*, won the Commonwealth Writers' Prize Best Book Award and was shortlisted for the Man Booker Prize in 2007.

Lloyd Jones lives in Wellington, New Zealand.

Here at the end of the world we learn to dance

Lloyd Jones

JOHN MURRAY

First published in Great Britain in 2008 by John Murray (Publishers)
An Hachette Livre UK company

1

© Lloyd Jones 2002

A CIP catalogue record for this title is
available from the British Library

ISBN 978-0-7195-2403-5

Typeset in Buccardi by Palimpsest Book Production Limited,
Grangemouth, Stirlingshire

Printed and bound by Clays Ltd, St Ives plc

John Murray policy is to use papers that are natural, renewable
and recyclable products and made from wood grown in
sustainable forests. The logging and manufacturing processes are
expected to conform to the environmental regulations of the
country of origin.

John Murray (Publishers)
338 Euston Road
London NW1 3BH

www.johnmurray.co.uk

'The tango is man and woman in search of each other.
It is a search for an embrace, a way to be together.'

JUAN CARLOS COPES,
CHOREOGRAPHER AND DANCER

– 1 –

FOR ELEVEN YEARS AN ELDERLY MAN WITH A SILVER-KNOBBED CANE VISITED
Louise's grave with flowers. He came every Saturday with a plastic
bucket, brush, cleaning fluids and a fold-up canvas chair. He was always
impeccably dressed for the occasion. A black blazer, white slacks.
A bright red flower in his buttonhole drew attention to his snow-
white hair.

The year before his death it was his habit to visit the *cementerio* at
Chacarita with his ten-year-old granddaughter. While he sat by Louise's
grave fanning his face with his fedora the granddaughter would go and
stand in line with her plastic bucket and the other mourners at the
water taps.

He had his own car, but for this particular excursion Paul Schmidt favoured the bus. The conductor helped him down the steps. He didn't experience any of the same uncertainty or hesitancy on the dance floor. He could always count on the same instruction, 'Careful of the traffic, Señor.' With a dismissive grunt Schmidt would set off across the busy road for the flower stand on Coronel Diaz.

For someone with a huge deception at the centre of his life, Schmidt prided himself on cultivating many small loyalties. That particular bus conductor, for instance. Another was the Paraguayan flower vendor from whom he always bought blue irises.

One Saturday morning a special flower of a competing vendor's display caught his eye — buttercup and broom — arousing in him an old memory. With some difficulty, as the bus was still moving, he stood out of his seat and stumbled past the knees of the woman sitting next to him. The bus lurched, and as his hands pawed at the dangling hand grips his cane clattered into the aisle. He didn't give it a second thought. Later, the conductor would recall Schmidt stooping to catch the receding view of the flowering broom in the back window, his hand on the shoulder of an unprotesting woman to steady himself.

At the next stop (not his usual stop) Schmidt struggled down the steps. The conductor caught up with him and handed him his cane. The old man gave it a brief regard and took it without thanks. The conductor smiled. They had an understanding, and in a manner of speaking had forged a friendship based on two predictable moments in each other's life. One, where the Señor picked up the bus and where he got off. The other significant moment arrived in the week leading up to Christmas when the Señor would give him a box of expensive cigars. It was always a last-minute thing. As the bus slowed down to his stop the cigars would be quickly produced and given without fuss as if he had no further use for them; for his part the conductor always received the cigars with noises of gratitude and false humility.

Now in the window of the bus he followed the old man's progress across the wide and busy road. He saw him poke his cane at the oncoming traffic. Later, the flower vendor would say that the Señor's 'eyes, face and memory were so closed around his flower display' (not merely the yellow flowering broom, note, but *his* flower display), 'that he did not see the bottle truck coming the other way'. Meanwhile, from the bus window a hollow warning rose in the conductor's throat. He closed his eyes to avoid the final moment of impact. It was a story he would tell many times. First, the distraction. The old man's sudden rush of blood to the head. Then, his wilfulness. The broken routine and — as a result — the loss of the cigars at Christmas.

– 2 –

At La Chacarita, the wealthy are laid to rest in huge pharaonic tombs; mausoleums are styled after famous chapels. Sculpted angels and lute-players pirouette in cement and plaster. Biblical scenes are lavishly carved out of stone. If a rich life must be seen to continue on into death the same could be said of the poor who are parked end to end, on top of one another, sandwiched into the massive walls of vaults. These older burial walls form inner walls of the *cementerio*. The newer vaults have been constructed by a mall developer. Bodies are stacked in galleria after galleria, and stairways descend two and three floors into the earth to work benches and cemetery workers in blue overalls shouldering brooms. The sickly fragrance is from the old flowers stuck in the coffin handles.

There was almost nothing that Schmidt could not have afforded. His widow had imagined a small family crypt, perhaps with some orchestral theme to symbolise the family business interests.

Instead, to his wife's great surprise, and the family's, Schmidt's final instructions were for a simple burial alongside his devoted shop assistant; a plain and quiet woman, the 'English woman' whom Señora Schmidt had known simply as Louise.

They had exchanged pleasantries. Proper conversation had always required extra effort. The woman's Spanish was at best infantile. When she shopped she pointed at the items she wanted, extending the word on the end of her finger. Now that Schmidt's wife tried to recall all those other times they had met the occasions were so brief that nothing particularly telling or revealing had stuck.

Once, during a summer storm, at her insistence Schmidt had dropped the 'shop assistant' off home in a taxi. She remembered glancing up at a grey building with a pink and blue plaster relief (a rosette, she seemed to recall) and the shop assistant's face suddenly dropping into the window to thank her for this kindness. Her hair was wet and unruly; her face washed out, a dark smear of eyeliner running from a corner of her eye. No one would ever say she was a classic beauty.

Louise had been dead for eleven years but one elderly woman, a former neighbour, remembered 'the English woman'. She recalled that she had kept to herself. The old woman shouted: 'She could not speak.' And no, she did not seek friendship. 'What about visitors? Did she have many?' The neighbour's face grew thoughtful. Schmidt's widow briefly considered offering money, but then the woman spoke: 'Many, no. Not many. But there was one . . .' And she began to describe her late husband, his shock of white hair, his smooth face, his chestnut eyes, the cane, his careful dress. 'You know how it is, Señora. Some people end their days having conquered time. Others are still running on the spot as they leave this world. The Señor was of the former category.' The conversation took place on the landing. A leaky tap could be heard along the way. It was such a rundown place. Her husband had always been so fussy. She couldn't place him here, on this landing. She began to walk along the hall. She stopped and looked back to check. 'This room at the end?' The woman nodded. 'Si, Señora, that is the room.' She thought, he must have seen this view, the same cold angling light in the end window, the same bare floorboards creaking under his feet. But what must he have felt? Excitement? A lift in his heart? The neighbour caught up with her. 'Señora, I can show you the courtyard if you wish. The gentleman and the foreign woman sometimes sat in the garden beneath the lime tree. The tree is no longer, I regret to say . . .'

Schmidt's widow shook her head. She had seen and heard enough. She was ready to leave. 'There is one other thing,' resumed the neighbour. She began to describe the day the landlord's men had shown up to cart away the dead woman's possessions. She suddenly looked mischievous and edged her face closer to confide. 'I snuck my head in for a look. I was curious too.' Well, there was little to remove. A record player, a stack of record albums, some articles of clothing, a pair of black stilettos, 'the kind worn by those who dance at the Ideal'. The widow had friends who danced there. Now she wondered if they had seen her husband with the shop assistant and chosen not to say anything. The neighbour continued. She was used to cluttered rooms herself, but in the dead woman's flat you noticed the floorboards. They stood out. Their long run and the 'scuff marks' in the middle of the main living area. The widow felt her eyes smart as she pushed out the next question, but she had to ask. 'She and the Señor liked to dance? Is this what you are telling me?' The neighbour made a grand display of her hands. 'Dance? They dance and they dance. Oh, how they dance. Then they sit in the garden to rest, then they dance some more. The woman did not speak. She dance only.'

– 3 –

No one passes through life unnoticed. The panaderia where she bought her bread sticks. The bus driver. The news-stand where she bought the English-language *Buenos Aires Herald*. And, of course, there was Max. Homosexual Max. His face tilted to receive kisses on both cheeks from his regulars. Max bulging like an overcooked soufflé inside his waiter's jacket. Max with his hairless chin. His small appreciative eyes glowing inside his spectacles. His body was found on the other side of Avenida Moreau de Justo in a stagnant pile of plastics and bottles, nudging against a bloated pig by the boatman's pier.

In the café where Max worked, small children with grown-up faces on the end of spindly bodies placed cigarette lighters on the tables of drinkers late in the afternoon. The drinkers waved them away like

14

blowflies. They tapped the ends of their cigarettes into the ashtrays and resumed their their thoughtful answers. A balding man, yes? No. No one could remember Max. For thirty years he worked behind the blinds at La Armistad, in the city neighbourhood of Montserrat, yet no one could remember his name.

Time is cruel, though necessarily so. The world has to make room for so many names.

In the 1940s, a young man with a large pink birthmark on his neck used to deliver coffee on a silver tray to Schmidt's staff on Coronel Diaz.

Years later the birthmark has faded and crumbled like an old head of agapanthus above a frayed and brackish collar. His eyes slope up to his crinkled forehead while he thinks back.

'Si. The Señora always ordered a short black.'

'A short black?'

'Si, espresso.'

'That is all?'

The man shrugged; his head and shoulders rose, his lips pursed; his eyes sloped down into the pit of memory.

'Sometimes a pastry,' he said.

'What kind of pastry?'

'Señora, it is a long time ago.'

Louise's friends, the ones she trusted and listened to and confided, day in, day out, year after year of lonely exile, are to be found in several rooms of a restored palace on Piedras and Independencia. Troilo. Goyeneche. Gardel. Each with their own room. You look up at the walls with their photographs. Their personal belongings are religiously displayed; on their own they are not particularly interesting — but that they belonged to Gardel is everything. So you find a long glass tube that contained the singer's toothbrush, his silver shoe-horn, a ring engraved with his image that the loving son gave to his French-born mother, his French-tailored collars, his cane, his silk *lengue*; and since the smallest detail is not to be overlooked, the ticket punch from window Number 10 where Gardel used to place his bets at the Palermo racecourse is included.

Then there are the photos. Gardel with his filmstar looks; his ever present smile, the slicked-back hair in the style he pioneered. In a group photograph you can tell which is Gardel simply by looking for the focal point. He is the one smiling his radiant smile, the grateful beneficiary of a once-in-a-century singing talent and universal love.

Louise arrived in Buenos Aires a few years before Gardel's plane crashed in Colombia. In all probability she was one of the hundreds of thousands who formed either side of his funeral procession up Corrientes to La Chacarita. The procession passed through the working-class neighbourhood of Almagro where she lived. She experienced this and other major historic events: the revolution, the war, the rise of Juan and Eva Perón, Evita's death and a funeral procession even larger than that which saw Gardel on his way. Defenders of Gardel's unimpeachable reputation are quick to point out that by the time of Eva's funeral, Buenos Aires had grown to a city four times the size it was in Gardel's day. In any case, these events are mere backdrop. They don't belong in Louise and Schmidt's story. The composers, the singers and the bandoneon players were more influential.

On the other hand, Gardel may have been a 'bit before her time', as they say. Gardel is best thought of as 'a friend of a friend', She and Paul Schmidt were closest in time and sensibility to Anibal Troilo and Goyeneche.

Troilo's original bandoneon sits behind glass in *la Troilo sala*. His signature piece 'Danzarin,' was a favourite. Of Louise's other friends, Julio Maria Sosa is represented by his Remington shaver, Sabina Olmos by her perfume bottles and Hugo Carril by his toiletries.

All those days and nights Schmidt was home tending to his other life, stoking the family coals, playing husband and father, Louise huddled next to her 1938 RCA Victor radio. The radio in the room next to Troilo's looks like a small beautiful wooden chapel.

– 4 –

ROSA IS THE NAME OF THE LITTLE GIRL WHO USED TO STAND IN LINE TO fill up the water bucket at La Chacarita.

She and her grandfather would catch the 39 at the corner of Paraguay and Coronel Diaz. The bus knew the way to the cemetery — they passed under the canopy of trees on Honduras, jumped the railway tracks with its tired rubbish, past the men spit-roasting meat under a scrap iron roof, past the markets. Before they turned up Maure on to Corrientes her grandfather would always look out the right-hand window for the two tenement buildings that stand like launch pads on a flattened landscape. The cemetery marked the end of the line for the bus route. After disembarking Rosa would gaze up at the grand entrance steps to the cemetery. It was like entering an opera house, elevated, and full of promise. The tug on her arm was her grandfather. She had forgotten to bring flowers. So from a florist on Guzman they would buy jasmine for Rosa to place on Gardel's tomb.

To a child, death is a story that is not quite believable. The crypts. The floating angels. The *cementerio* workers. The ones in green to collect the leaves. The ones in blue with mops and buckets to wash down the steps of the huge, ostentatious family tombs. On a summer's morning Rosa would peek down the shadowed stairs to a shrine of light. Impossible to imagine that something as small as a flower urn might contain a whole life. And once, when she saw an admirer light a cigarette for the famous singer's bronzed hand, she understood that Gardel was not quite as dead as everyone made out.

It was the bit afterwards she looked forward to — after her grandfather had finished with washing his old shop assistant's headstone — when they repaired to El Imperio de la Pizza. Nothing has changed. Today the café sprawls onto two busy avenues. The doors are flung open to catch the diesel fumes and the occasional whiff of fresh air.

Rosa and Schmidt always sat at the same table with the view out the doors across Avenida Corrientes to the palms outside the grand entrance to the *cementerio*. The old man would ease into his chair as though he'd deemed it to be his final resting place. One massive sigh and his face became immobilised. For several long minutes Rosa would divert her attention to the huge metal fans beating inside the wire cages; sitting patiently and respectfully until her grandfather's face twitched and sputtered into a smile. 'Did I drop off? No. Did I snore? I didn't snore, did I?' About now the oldest waiter would decide to look up to discover them and approach with a smile in the maw of his broken teeth.

He and Schmidt always greeted each other warmly. As with his bus conductor and the flower vendor, Schmidt remembered *his* waiter at Christmas. One year the waiter hobbled to the table with their pizza, complaining of arthritis in his hip. His scooter needed repairs which he couldn't afford. It meant he had to walk to El Imperio. After the old man limped away with his silver tray, that day, along with his usual tip, Schmidt left an envelope with the money needed to cover the repairs. Rosa had watched her grandfather count out the notes until he caught her eye. Placing a finger to his lips, he said, 'Not a word to your grandmother.'

The trips to La Chacarita were to end with her grandfather's death. Thereafter, her grandmother led her on a wild-goose chase all across the city. Whole days were spent getting in and out of taxis to look up at old houses with dusty windows. 'This is where your grandfather and I lived in 1926 . . . This is where we liked to go on Sundays for lunch . . . This is the apartment where I was pregnant with your father . . .'

But this landscape was even harder to believe in than the statuary of the cemetery.

The warehouse where her grandfather opened his first store was now, inexplicably, a *parrilla*. Rosa stared in the window and listened to her grandmother place the tubas, pianos, bandoneons, and guitars. Eventually an irritated diner would stop mid-sentence or mid-mouthful to glower back and off they'd go, to stand outside the next address. A café, a dress shop, a furniture store, all were once part of the family's empire of musical instrument stores. Now the landscape lay trans-formed. It did not remember. Those parts of her marriage she wished to retrieve had vanished under the new layers. So the city too had betrayed her.

Inevitably they would end up outside the last remaining store run by Schmidt's son, a comparatively dull and unimaginative man. His sole outside interest was the Almagro football team. Michael Schmidt and music were not a natural fit. But like his father he was a generous man who found it impossible to deny his daughter. So after arriving back at the shop Rosa would run to her father and beg for sweets, leaving the old woman to stand alone and stare at the family name SCHMIDT cast in gold-embossed dark lettering across the windowfront.

Her grandmother repeated the same story over and over. She was nineteen years old when she answered an advertisement for a shop clerk. She had never known anyone to work so hard as her grandfather. 'It was like someone making up for lost time.'

'And of course his Spanish was scratchy.'

This was the most surprising thing she had heard about her grandfather. It was perhaps the third or fourth time she was hearing this story that she raised the courage to ask why her Poppa's Spanish was, as she put it, 'scratchy'.

'He was from Bournemouth. His father was a glassblower.'

'So he was English?'

'Well, Schmidt is a German name, isn't it.'

The old woman grew impatient reciting these facts, as if they were already known.

'His father was German. A German glassblower. Your Poppa was a piano tuner when he emigrated.' The old woman glanced away. Her face closed on a half-forgotten memory of the shop assistant. She added, 'Everyone has to come from somewhere, Rosa. Even butterflies.'

On one of these outings Rosa left her grandmother sitting on a bench to go and buy an ice-cream. It was a hot December afternoon and quite a crowd gathered around the ice-cream vendor. When she looked back she saw her grandmother had grown tired of waiting. She was resting on her side. By the time Rosa returned to the bench the old woman was asleep, so she sat beside her eating her ice-cream. Vanilla with fancy strawberry whorls. Her favourite. She finished it, licked her fingers and waited. She waited until she decided her grandmother had slept long enough. 'Nanna, wake up. Nanna, it is time to go.' She pulled on her grandmother's sleeve. She picked up her arm. When she let it go it flopped back into place. A young man, an unemployed schoolteacher in a frayed suit, stopped. He spoke softly to Rosa, then crouched next to the old woman's head. After checking her pulse he released a slow whistling breath between his lips. He looked at Rosa, clucked his tongue. He reached in his pocket for a sweet which she unwrapped and ate. Strawberry and banana. Who would have thought . . .

Death kept throwing up new surprises.

The old woman was buried in La Chacarita. And, as if to go one up on the shop assistant, she left instructions for her remains to rejoin her husband's. Since they had hardly spent a single night apart while alive, she saw no reason to change this arrangement in death, even if it meant putting up with the 'other woman' alongside them. The epitaph on her headstone reads: *In death as in life.*

— 5 —

LOOK CLOSELY ENOUGH AND YOU CAN FIND THE CHILD IN THE ADULT AND
vice versa. The child whose requests for ice-cream and pony rides
Schmidt could never refuse, and who once cried when her parents
painted her bedroom blue without first consulting her, is also the
woman with the flaming black eyes and stubborn legs whose way of
saying, 'I see there isn't a table cloth on table six!' would result in a
panic among the waitresses in their rush to correct the oversight.

I was nineteen years old, newly arrived in the city, a student in need
of a part-time job. Rosa was thirty-six. To this day I cannot think of
Rosa without her holding a cigarette in her hand. I can summon the tilt
of her chin just before she releases a smoke ring to the ceiling. The
space above her head was always layered in cloud. She smoked when it

23

was no longer fashionable to do so. No one I knew smoked. We drank, but in our new enlightenment we didn't touch cigarettes. In Rosa's case you felt an exception could be made. It was forgivable because she was foreign, and it was because she was foreign that she smoked. A cigarette was as vital to her sense of self as the lush red lipstick she heavily applied. Rosa's looks and her accented English — a casual mix of flat Australian vowels (a result of her family shifting to Sydney when she was eighteen) and some darker traces of something else, Italian, Spanish — or whatever they spoke in the Argentine (I didn't know then) — was also part of La Chacra's appeal. Rosa was foreign. And foreign restaurants were the happening thing. La Chacra was first to serve up sour cream with potatoes in their jackets. The salad came separately in a bowl. No one commented on these little differences. It was chic to pretend that this was the way we had always eaten salad. La Chacra's salads also contained flowers. I'd find the crushed flowers set aside on the bowls that reached me back in the kitchen. Others placed them in their mouths and closed their eyes and hoped that they were doing the right thing, that they weren't setting in train a future event that would see a primrose grow out their arse. The other thing about La Chacra was the music. Argentine music. Tango music. 'Mi Buenos Aires Querido'. 'Adios Muchachos'. 'Tomo y Obligo'. 'Mi Noche Triste'. 'Viejo Rincon'. All are tango standards made famous by Gardel in the first half of the last century but still available today, in Buenos Aires, on just about any tango compilation.

I first heard them in the late hours scrubbing pots and pans. Troilo, Gardel and Goyeneche were background noise — a bandoneon now, and then a honeyed voice on the edge of a garrulous crowd as the

Anglophone diners sawed through their Steaks Argentine and shouted at one another across a table littered with empty chianti bottles dripping candlewax.

The last hour of a dishwasher's shift is the worse. It drags on for ever. The minute hand on the clock seems held back by some invisible force. Then, when your battery is at its lowest, the pans suddenly pile up and keep on coming until it seems like there will be no end to them. To make things worse, the waitresses are getting into their coats and it's hard not to feel for yourself as the last of them yells 'ciao' and runs out to the car where their boyfriend is waiting. This was also the hour when the restaurant would go into another little shift that few others knew about. Rosa would turn up the stereo, and at the first heart-breaking bars of 'Mi Buenos Aires Querido' I'd soon forget that I was actually scrubbing pans and feeding the dishwasher. I'd forget all that and bury myself in these wonderful pick-and-strum tango melodies which eventually I'd come to know and sing along to.

I'd been there a week, and in that time I'd seen Rosa sack a waitress for turning up late once too often. I'd seen her throw a temper tantrum after a huge party she'd gone out of her way for — buying in more provisions and laying on two extra waitresses — phoned in to cancel (she sacked the waitresses later that same night) and I'd learnt to keep my head down and to make sure I wiped the benches and left the kitchen looking spic and span. I hadn't spoken more than two words to Rosa, but all that was about to change.

It was another mid-week night, and after dumping my soiled apron in the wash pile, I came out to the front of the restaurant to find Rosa dancing with her cigarette. She had her back to me. Still, I could make out the circling notion of her arms; the glowing end of her cigarette approximating the distance of a dance partner. That is what she was doing. She was dancing. I wished she wasn't because it was such a private moment, and because of that I had it framed in my mind as a potentially dangerous one. Rosa wouldn't like to be caught out. However, if I was quick about it I could slip out the door without her noticing, saving her embarrassment and me my job.

That's what I was about to do when she glanced back over her shoulder and without any of the humiliation or embarrassment that I had imagined she would feel, that I would have felt in her place, for a brief moment she looked at me as if she was trying to recollect who I was. Most of the time Rosa had the nervy energy of a blackbird in a hedge. All eyes and breast and twitchy feet. With a cigarette she became imperious, a raven-haired Catherine the Great. Judgment rushed into her face. Her eyes narrowed as they did now. Her gaze shifted over to the door, and immediately she seemed to know what I had been thinking. She gave a short snort — as if she'd just come to an appreciation of the facts that separated our lives: she was thirty-six years old, married, and I was a nineteen-year-old improvident student. She was the restaurant owner and manager. I was the dishwasher. These differences came and went as she placed the cigarette back in her mouth and waved me over — then it was like any other instruction that passes between the boss and the hired help.

'I need to dance,' she said.

I thought she was just airing that thought in a general and speculative kind of way. I didn't think it necessarily included me. But then she snapped her fingers, and gestured for me to join her.

'I can't,' I said.

She gave me an odd look.

'I can't dance,' I explained.

'Everyone can dance.'

'Not me.'

'So, are you carrying an injury?'

'No,' I said.

'Perhaps you are sick?'

'No, Rosa, I'm not sick.'

'So you *can* dance.' Already she was looking for a place to put down her cigarette.

I had no choice. She slipped inside my dishwasher arms with a little smile of triumph.

'Thank you, Pasta.'

That was the other new thing that happened to me. A nickname, bestowed on me by Angelo, the chef, in acknowledgment of my huge appetite for pasta.

'Put your arms around.'

I did what she asked; I could feel her smoky breath on my face.

'Right around and behind,' she instructed. 'The Argentine way is to dance closer. The other way it is like two people carrying a water tank between them. I do not care for that.'

'Mi Noche Triste' was playing. She hummed to that while she waited — and waited.

She spoke into my ear. She whispered.

'You are not doing anything.'

'I told you I can't dance.'

'Everyone can dance.'

'I can't.'

Rosa wasn't one to let a slight inconvenience get in the way of what she wanted. We parted so she could make the necessary adjustments. 'I want you to bend your knees. Not too much. Just so.' She looked into my eyes to see what was residing there. I felt her hand adjust my chin. 'You are not relaxed. How are you to dance if you are not relaxed? Breathe!' she commanded. I breathed. 'Good. Well, better. Now you are starting to relax, I can tell.' She instructed me to place my hands on her shoulders and to walk her backwards. And once when I looked down, she asked me, 'Have you dropped something? Did you hear something roll on to the floor? No. So why are you looking down?'

'Sorry.'

'There is no need to be. You are just beginning.'

And then, 'Now you are trying to walk around me. Walk like you want to walk through me. If you kick me it is my fault. No problem.'

I seriously wondered about that. I had seen her sack a waitress for much less, for what had seemed little more than wilfulness on Rosa's part. I wasn't relaxed. I was extremely nervous.

'Wait,' she said, and detached herself to dispose of her cigarette. She looked back from the table and smiled as if she had just caught up with the fact of my clumsy youthfulness.

'Lionel, you are still not completely relaxed, are you?'

'No.'

'So how can you dance if you are not relaxed? Come.'

She eyeballed my hands and smiled when I woodenly raised them

28

for her to step back inside my embrace. We were close enough now for me to feel her thighs on mine. Her breasts pushed up against my ribcage. On the beat I began to walk her backwards. To my surprise it worked. Rosa was a receding obstacle. She moved with surprising lightness. In fact, she moved expertly. Happily, for me, 'Almagro' was the last track on the tape, and as it ended we found ourselves by the reception where she released me.

I could hear the tape whirring over the speakers. I thought for a moment she would put another tape on. Instead she looked vaguely over towards the bar.

She said, 'I'm going to have a glass of wine. Would you like something?'

I made a thing of looking at my watch. It was already late. But that wasn't the problem I made it out to be. Sheepishly I told her I had an early morning lecture which while true was neither here nor there. Even to my ears it sounded unconvincing, and before I could change tack Rosa was walking towards the door.

'Of course,' she said. 'You must go. It is late. Look at what time it is and I'm holding you up. Go.'

She had walked quickly, much too quickly; now she waited at the door for me to leave.

In the short time that I had been the kitchenhand rumours about the state of Rosa's marriage had made the rounds. When the waitresses came back to smoke and gossip in the loading bay I'd hear Ivan referred to. A couple of times I was still cleaning up when he swung by the restaurant to pick up Rosa. The first time I was bringing out Angelo's pans when I saw him hovering near the door. I was surprised not so much by what he was or looked like but what he didn't look like. I had expected someone older. Or by that do I mean someone more confident? Someone who wouldn't be shy of leading Rosa around the dance floor. Ivan wore a shapeless woolly jumper. His hands slumped in his pockets. His sideburns were too bushy. One glance at shambling Ivan and you knew why the running of the restaurant was left to Rosa. He looked uncomfortable to be there. A man given to complaint, I thought then.

Rosa looked up from her little adding machine, saw me, and called out across the empty restaurant: 'Say hallo to our new kitchenhand. His name is Lionel.' Ivan raised his hand and looked away. He really didn't want to know. He just wanted to get out of there. He jangled change in his pocket while he waited for Rosa to lock up. But she couldn't do that until I had finished out the back. In the meanwhile she was gentle and solicitous with him. 'Ivan, why don't you sit down and have a drink? Lionel will be done by the time you've finished. Why don't you pour yourself a brandy? Or a soda or something?'

Ivan just shrugged and jangled change in his pocket.

Then there was a period when I didn't see him at all. We all assumed he was waiting up at home, planted before the TV or in bed. Ivan was referred to less and less. I'd been there a month when one night a waitresses came back to say that Rosa had left Kay in charge while she drove Ivan out to the airport. We took that to mean that the marriage was over. Ivan was flying back to Melbourne. Or was it Sydney? Someone said Ivan ran with some Yugoslav crooks. Ivan had come to mean bad business. So we were all relieved for Rosa's sake that she'd finally pulled this sick thorn from her side.

A weather watch went out on Rosa. Everyone figured this would not be a good time to ask Rosa for any favours or to be late. We were expecting a fire storm. So it was a surprise to find Rosa more subdued; well, we figured that was also to be expected. It was over, and even if it had been a bad marriage (we'd decided that was the case) a certain amount of grieving was understandable. Kay, who was the oldest waitress (she may have been as old as thirty-two) set the tone by speaking in a hush and generally moving about as though in an intensive care ward. She'd been through a marriage break-up herself. 'Believe me, once is enough.' Her quiet efficient manner carried through to the kitchen. Plates were placed delicately rather than dropped in a pile. Angelo would come all the way down to my sink rather than yell out to ask when he could have the meat pan back.

Some things continued the same as before. The low dismal cloud of smoke hanging over Rosa. When I stopped to say goodnight she forced herself to smile, parted with a quick 'Good night, Pasta' and went back to her adding machine. I found myself wishing that I'd accepted that offer of a drink. I should have just swallowed my nerves and gone with the moment. Because the other thing that had happened, and it was something I wanted to draw to Rosa's attention, was the music. For whatever reason she'd stopped turning it up after the last waitress ran out at the stroke of midnight. So that final hour I spent scrubbing without the salve of Troilo, Gardel and Goyeneche.

I resolved to mention this and one night as I was leaving I called across to Rosa in her booth. I said, 'What's happened to the music, Rosa? I miss it.'

31

She kept looking down at her figures, her whispering lips moved to the end of the adding machine printout. It was only a matter of seconds but I felt like I'd interrupted her with some unforgivable triviality. Finally, she looked up and studied me through the grey smoke.

'What you want? You want to dance?'

'Yes,' I said. Though this wasn't true. I didn't mean that. I just missed the music.

Still, I would have thought she would be pleasantly surprised to hear this. Instead, her expression didn't change at all. She just ground out her cigarette in an ash-tray. A boy at primary school used to sit on the hot asphalt and grind red ants to a pulp under his fingertip. Rosa rotated her finger the same way and with the same relish when she ground out a cigarette.

'Well,' she said, after what was a drawn-out consideration. 'I don't think so.' That was all she said. She stuck a new cigarette in her mouth and felt around in the coils of adding machine paper for her lighter. The matter was apparently at an end. So I nodded back. That was fine with me. Better in fact. It was a huge relief. I'd done the right thing. Now I could go. 'However,' she said. 'If you are interested . . .'

The blackbird in the hedge suddenly stopped twiching; its eyes glowed back at me.

'Yes,' I heard myself say.

'Then you will need to take some lessons. The lessons I can arrange and then, perhaps I will dance with you.'

– 6 –

THE WHITE LIGHTS, THE LONG BROWN FLOORBOARDS. THE SOFT PASTEL
reflections of the dancers catching on the dark glass. Dancers finding a
place to sit and change out of their street shoes, then standing to press
their weight into every corner of their shoes. One foot, then the other.
The men less experimental, more in a hurry to tie their shoelaces. One
man's eyes glinted madly behind his glasses; the jaw of another set with
canine anticipation. I watched a number of women step forward from
the fringes; like reluctant swimmers, wanting, desiring, but not quite
trusting. Big women in heavy lipstick and in dresses that were too short.
Skinny ones who held their hands in front of themselves and looked
much like they must have once behind a school desk.

This scene repeated itself in dance classes across the city.

33

My first lesson was in a small school hall off a road leading to the rubbish dump. This was in early spring. I got off a bus full of sneezing people, and as I crossed a tennis court, I could smell the gorse on the hills. I glanced up at the puffy white clouds. Everything spoke of lightness. But because of the heat it didn't feel like either the right time of day or the right time of the year to be taking a dance lesson.

A single car, a Lada, was parked on the tennis court. It occurred to me that I had the wrong school or the wrong time. Either possibility would have been fine. I'd tell Rosa that I'd got the time wrong. And the idea of dance lessons would slowly fade.

That's when I heard the first sad bars of 'Milonga Triste' tumble out the doorway of the school hall.

There is something undeniably sad about accordion music (out of German or Austrian hands, I mean) and especially in an empty hall. It makes a mockery of empty spaces. It puts you in mind of a phoney civic occasion created for a South American despot.

As I stood in the doorway, accordion music sweeping towards me, I took in a scary fact. I was the only dancer. The one other in the hall beaming at me, a short, dark-haired man in black trousers and a white buttoned-down shirt, must be Mr Hecht. Rosa had given me his contact details. We'd spoken on the phone and he'd managed to ease some of my fears. I told him I was a beginner.

'No problem.'

'No, but I'm a seriously bottom-of-the-class beginner.'

'So is everyone when they first start.'

'I've never danced, you know.'

'We try and cater for all levels.'

34

Nothing I said was a surprise to him. When I mentioned Rosa's name, and what a good dancer I thought she was, all he said was, 'Rosa can dance.'

Mr Hecht glanced up. He looked at his watch. 'You're in luck,' he said. 'Usually half a dozen turn up for this class.'

I didn't feel lucky. Where were they all? I wanted a crowd.

We waited a few more minutes. Mr Hecht played around with his tape deck. He experimented with a number of tapes. Voice/instrumental/back to voice. Then he too looked around the hall as if the others might be hiding underneath the chairs. On one of these inspections he discovered my feet. I thought I saw him wince.

I was in the same sneakers I wore every day, to my lectures, to wash dishes at the restaurant. Mr Hecht ran a finger across his lip, then darted out to his car, the Lada parked on the tennis court. He came back with a pair of hand-made Brazilian boots for me. They were black leather, soft and pursy, with zips up the sides, and squeaked when I walked.

I squeaked out to the middle of the floor where we began with some stretches. We both kept stealing glances at the door — I caught him once and he smiled at me and said, 'Very unusual.' Another time a car drove in off the street and turned around on the tennis court. A face looked speculatively towards the open door and we looked speculatively back and the car drove off again. 'Well, I suppose we might as well begin.' I thought he sounded a touch regretful.

Some of what he had to say was already familiar. Rosa had stressed the need for flex in the knees. Now I followed Mr Hecht on the 'tightrope' walk, ankles and knees brushing, the toe of the extended foot probing for the floor ahead. We walked up and down the hall like that for several minutes, sliding, open-hipped, thrusting forward. I couldn't stop smiling at my silky self. 'This time with your eyes closed,' said Mr Hecht and immediately I felt my balance go. I righted the ship and started off again, frontwards and backwards, until a word of caution from Mr Hecht found me a step away from crashing into the chairs along the side of the hall. Now he introduced a step to the side. So the movement was one step back, one step across. He moved to his left and I followed. The dance instructor and his hesitant shadow.

I left the hall with the pleasant hazy feeling of achievement. Of course, for the entire lesson all I'd done was place my feet in the spaces left by the dance instructor. It wasn't like I'd had to lead anyone.

The true test came the following Sunday night. In a narrow hall, home to an Immigration Advisory Service during the week, I found myself partnering a girl my own age. She had lovely olive skin. She could have been from Tunisia or Malta. She wore blue tights. A brief cotton top bubbled with her breasts and left her midriff bare. A body piercing flashed goldenly near her navel. The first time she smiled up at me I saw a wad of white gum in her teeth. The bit of chewing gum turned out to be an integral part of her communicative effort. It was quite sweet really. Once, when by some fluke the music and a nicely judged turn neatly cohered, her eyes lit up; she drew her lips to dangle the white thread of gum, and I felt rewarded.

At the restaurant another routine established itself. After the last waitress had left — it was usually Kay — and after I'd finished up in the kitchen, Rosa would invite me to show her what I'd learnt and then make the necessary adjustments to the steps I'd imperfectly picked up.

A moment's hesitation on my part would sometimes cause us to stall. Rosa's response depended on the length of delay, or the extent to which I'd become stuck. If I quickly got us moving again there would be a grunt of approval. But when the solution didn't come swiftly enough she would lean back, her face brimming with circular inquiry, and if I was still at a loss she would treat me to that doleful look of someone waiting for their correct change from a complete idiot on the other side of the counter.

She tolerated these surrenders at the start, patiently explaining that there was no correct answer. Beyond the solid foundation of the *ocho* there was no 'lawful sequence', as she put it. To stall just gave you away. It revealed an 'arid imagination', she said, or as I preferred and which was probably closer to the truth, a lack of confidence to express myself so intimately. I was off a farm. The bare hills and the wind — these were my companions. Dogs and sheep, and the sleepy-lidded sky. I wasn't used to people so close up. Intimacy was a faraway notion. I had no experience of it, and because of that I recognised there was a line for me to cross — a line that separated private and public, containment and abandonment, secrecy and expression.

For all that, Rosa had opened the door to something new. The *gancha*, and the equally sexy 'sandwich' step. These days I found myself drifting to a different part of the library. In the margins of my notes on economic history I found myself jotting down new bits of information — '*que brada* : an improvised jerky contortion, the more dramatic the better'

'*corte* : a sudden, suggestive pause' (a prelude to *que brada*)

'that reptile from the brothel' (a reference to the tango in *El Payador* newspaper)

37

'What was once orgiastic devilry is now just another way of walking . . .' (Borges)

'Tangos are spectacular confessions. They are public displays of intimate miseries, shameful behaviour, and unjustifiable attitudes . . .' (Savigliano)

And this, what an Argentine poet had to say about the 'famous' La Moreira who lived with her *criollo* pimp. 'There was no marriage contract, only constant seduction.'

This was new air I was breathing. Much of my life up to then involved a world I had known in advance of actually experiencing it. School. University. Sports. Drunkenness. I put a tick in each box as I came to it. Rosa represented a different kind of eddy. She was foreign and an entirely unexpected element in my life. What's more, the dance lessons and the shabby halls represented a world that hadn't been officially sanctioned. It's possible that I liked the idea of taking dance lessons more than the actual lessons themselves. To begin with that was probably true. But at some point a genuine interest kicked in. I found myself more interested; interested in Rosa as well. And although I wasn't aware of it at the time I was also taking the first steps towards hearing the story of Schmidt and Louise.

It began predictably enough with a bit of criticism. Rosa said I didn't give anything to my steps. They lacked heart and conviction. I might as well be putting out the milk bottles. No. Forget the milk bottles. She said, 'It is as though you are swimming underwater. Every so often you rise to the surface and lunge for a breath. Your face is practically changing colour. You are drowning before my eyes.' Then, less dramatically, 'Lionel, watch, I am going to teach you to breathe.' Rosa advanced her foot and as she moved her weight forward she exhaled. 'Yes?' 'Yes,' I said. 'So, perhaps we will practise our breathing . . . Give me your hand. We will walk to the end tables . . .' That's what we did, hand in hand, pressing my leading toe into the carpet, driving it there with an exhalation. 'We are exaggerating, of course,' she said. 'But the breath will help give shape and character to how we dance. One last thing, please. When you breathe out aim down at the floor. Not that I am worried.'

The next night we have finished one dance and are waiting to begin another when Rosa says, 'Still, technique is just part of it. You can learn that inside a month, frankly. But to learn the feeling . . . well, that can take years. A lifetime to learn.' She must have noted the deflating effect of this news because she followed up quickly with a more encouraging timeframe. She said, 'If you haven't fallen in love by the end of the dance you haven't danced the tango.'

'One dance?' I said. Even by Rosa's standards this was extravagant. 'One dance might only be three minutes.'

'Or shorter.'

'Or longer.'

'Yes. Possibly. Of course, as the case may be.'

'Three minutes to fall in love?'

I was feeling more secure in my employment these days so I didn't try to hide my scepticism.

'This is a fact,' she said.

'Oh, a fact. So you can prove it? After all a fact is . . .'

39

'I know what a fact is, Lionel. And I know it to be true because it has happened.'

'To you?'

'No,' she said carefully. 'Not to me . . .'

She pursed her lips, ready to say more but some other thought intruded and had a cautioning effect. Her attention shifted to Table 14. Her expression changed to annoyance. 'Lionel, is that a dinner plate I see left out?'

Mr Hecht had been Rosa's idea. For no reason other than to show my independence I felt I had to seek out another teacher.

Harry Singer, a cyclist and retired greengrocer, gave lessons in a studio above an Indian restaurant. Harry worked with another, younger teacher, a foreigner, Frederico, who took the more seasoned dancers.

Whereas Mr Hecht was precise in his movements and description, Harry was like the elderly shopkeeper he had once been, dashing back and forth between the shelves and his counter. 'Okay. We'll try this . . . Watch . . .' His hands pawed the air for a partner. He wasn't good at remembering names, but if he stared long enough and looked flustered in the right direction, sooner or later a woman would detach herself from Frederico's group and drag herself up the leper's end of the hall.

'Right. I want you to do this. Like this. Walk behind me.'

I became the third dancer, the shadow at the grocer's back, tracing out his steps, his bony head looking back over his shoulder, correcting me. 'Like this,' he'd say. In this copy-me style of Harry's I learned the *gancha* where the woman flicks her heel inside your forward-thrust leg. Harry had a warning: 'Some don't like it. Personally I don't mind, so long as she doesn't use my trousers to wipe her shoes.' This remark produced a nervous twitter.

Harry also introduced a rock 'n' roll spin, a move of his own, and nothing to do with tango, as I discovered. He demonstrated with Diane, a short blonde woman with a wonderfully reassuring voice and manner. 'I can't believe this is your first time,' she said. Of course I had lied. And once, as I spun her inside the arc of my arm, she actually applauded. 'Good. Very good. I'll dance with you any time.' Harry wasn't happy, though. His arms were folded. His face hung disapprovingly. 'That last spin,' he said, 'it happened too far away. Keep your hand flat against the back and let them spin around it.' He and Diane demonstrated and Harry's hand rode around her back, waist, round to the front. He winked. 'Once you've got them there you don't let them get away.'

I tried to introduce the move to Rosa, and as I went to spin her I felt her resist. From the half turn where we had stalled she gave me a look of incomprehension. 'What is this? What is this you are trying to do?' It was as though I'd made an improper suggestion. She picked my hand off her.

I didn't want to mention the retired grocer's lessons. I didn't want her to think I had been elsewhere, 'behind her back', or that I didn't have confidence in her judgment or Hecht as a dance instructor.

She looked at me suspiciously.

'Just improvising,' I said.

'You may improvise. Sure, that is the tango. But perhaps wait until you've learnt the steps. Yes?'

41

'Yes.'

We went back to the *ocho* and the square-on body position, followed by another lecture which completely contradicted the retired grocer's take on gender relations. 'You must not imprison the woman but you may exert force, yes.' We moved off to 'Los Argentinos'. Just as quickly Rosa stopped. 'Look in to my eyes. You are not looking.'

'I thought I was.'

'No. You were not.'

'I thought . . .'

'So you want to argue with a mirror?'

I shut up.

She said, 'If you look past my shoulder you will lose your balance.' Intimacy, as it was explained to me, was a practical matter and nothing to be afraid of.

When I wasn't washing dishes I was in the library reading or in my room back at the hostel writing assignments. That part of my life doesn't belong to the events I'm about to describe. It barely intrudes. Except for this. Coming into October and end-of-the year finals I didn't really have enough time or money for dance lessons. I missed one lesson, then another. A further week slipped by without a dance lesson. Whenever Rosa asked me how the lessons were coming on it was easy and convenient to say, 'Fine.' But that lie was exposed the moment I led her around the restaurant floor. She wasn't seeing the improvement she might have expected. I had stalled, and she was puzzled by this after all the 'earlier promise' I'd shown. She was also used to hearing more detail about the odd places that hosted the lessons. The Irish Club, for example. The walk past the outside urinals. The white fibrolite ceiling and the stencilled sign outside the door: 'No drinking past this point.' The dance lessons gypsied around town. Church halls. The Community Arts Centre where a gay Indian sat in the lotus position instructing his young female charges on graceful movement. The Irish Club had its cloverleaf — embroidered hockey sticks and fiddles over the walls. The yoga centre. The Centre for Refugees. Dance, it seemed, didn't have a specific place to call its own.

Rosa was also a wicked gossip. She loved to hear descriptions of the women I danced with. Her eyes gleamed when I mentioned the bossy 'Dutch woman' who, tired of my preoccupied eyes, had stopped while we were dancing and detached herself to ask, 'Are you dancing with me or the wall behind?' Rosa liked that. It was her choice to scoff or take sides. Naturally, she saw the Dutch woman's point of view. She said, 'A woman does not want to feel like she is a lamppost heaved from one place to the other.' Another woman with sour breath ticked me off for always looking down at my feet. Halfway through my account she interrupted me. 'As you know, as I have told you already, that is vulgar, Lionel. But then so is sour breath. So it is difficult for me to have an opinion.' She was curious all the same. 'What exactly did her breath smell of?' I recalled, 'Kind of metallic, like she hadn't opened her mouth for a month.' She was delighted. *Too* delighted. That only encouraged me more.

There was one woman who after we managed a smooth transition out of a forward *ocho* hooted like she might have at a well-taken goal.

There was Glenda who apologised in advance. She pointed to a man with a tousled beard, her husband. 'He's the dancer,' she said. It was 'Bob' from Somerset. Once when there was a shortage of women

43

I'd danced with him. We'd practised the rocking motion together. 'So who's wearing the shirt?' he asked. Obviously they didn't dance together much. The toe of my advancing foot kept banging into hers. The more we collided the more she swore in a panicky way. 'Shit, shit,' and with mounting panic, 'Shit, shit, shit!' and as I kept marching her backwards: 'Shit. Shit. Shit.'

As far as Rosa went I must have given the impression of an enthusiast, a regular attendee at classes, *practica,* and dances stacked throughout the week. In truth, I had strayed. Study was taking up more and more of my time. I didn't mention this to Rosa. Whenever she asked after the lessons and I gave my stock answer she raised her eyebrow. There are many ways of saying, 'I don't believe you,' and Rosa seemed to know them all.

I didn't want to fail her, so in need of a new step to report back with, I turned up to one of Mr Hecht's workshops at the tramping club in Moncrief Street.

Everyone looked so competent. Many of the faces were familiar. I was pleased to see a large woman who I'd caused some anxiety at another practica smiling at her partner, a slim man in a white shirt and black tie. I'd seen him before as well, a Czech poet taxi driver who'd written a script for a dance film about a man and a woman who meet under a clothesline while hanging out their clothes (at least, that's what I'd been told). I 'd seen him sitting in his taxi outside various venues across town, waiting for the lesson to start; once he was in a black leather jacket licking a vanilla ice-cream, and I'd thought, isn't that like a Czech poet. I switched my attention to Mr Hecht. He was demonstrating a step that was new to me. He switched on the music and everyone managed to remember what they'd been shown, except me. I seemed to be the only one incapable of remembering the pattern. I gazed back at the end wall. A pair of wooden skis were nailed up there in the shape of a crucifix. I decided to sit down.

I was reading the list of names on the tramping club's honours board when Mr Hecht crept up on me.

'Lionel, this is Brenda. Brenda, Lionel.'

I stood up and apologised in advance of the coming disaster.

'I'm sure you will be fine,' said Brenda.

She thought I was being bashful. But as we walked out to rejoin the others on the dance floor she began to have misgivings. She said, 'You have danced the *milonga* before, haven't you?' The *milonga* is a faster dance than the tango. More complex. Before she could turn and run for the doors the music started. 'Buenos Aires Conoce'. She was built so delicately it was like holding a twig. With the others I'd managed a few confident steps before the wheels fell off. With Brenda we stopped, we started, we stopped. I said I was sorry. She said it was her. It was really me, though. I couldn't lead. She tried to blame herself. 'No, I'm leading and shouldn't be.'

Brenda was my last dance in the tramping club. In fact, she was my last paid dance.

There was one other memorable moment which I told Rosa about. It came as the music stopped and Mr Hecht told everyone to keep dancing. Then you heard the shuffling and scraping sound of soles on floorboards. If you listened carefully you heard the shape and rhythm of dance. It is the sound of a hand crushing rice paper.

45

'It is also the sound of the tide moving in and out.'

I stopped. I wasn't sure I had heard correctly. I looked back at Rosa. Her expression was that of someone who has let out an indiscretion. A light colouring entered her face. She was reflecting on what she'd just said, and for the moment she appeared to teeter between backtracking and disowning the remark or explaining further. Her movements became very deliberate. After a suck on her cigarette she ground it out.

'The tide. You were about to say,' I said.

Her gaze was still aimed away from me. I had never seen Rosa like this before, defensive and indecisive. When she looked up and met my eye I realised that she still hadn't quite made up her mind about me.

'Well,' she said. 'To properly explain I will need to introduce you to some people.'

For a moment I thought she meant more colleagues, like Hecht. But, no. She drew herself up from her booth and signalled me to follow.

We crossed the restaurant to the wall of photos displayed behind the cash register. I had seen them before but only in passing.

This was the first time I heard the names of Louise Cunningham and Paul Schmidt.

We looked up at an older Buenos Aires, sepia-coloured, stained with age, full of swept courtyards and flowering balconies. Rosa pointed to a woman astride a bike, her feet planted firmly on the ground. 'This is Louise,' she said. In that photo she was a woman in her thirties. Sunglasses; a jersey tied casually around her neck. Her blonde hair swept back in a scarf. In another, taken outside a café, she appears so much older it was hard to believe they were the same person. A cardigan is draped lightly about her shoulders. The photo is

46

half in shadow. The light is drawn to her chin, and on closer inspection she is smiling up from under the brim of her hat. This photo was retrieved from Schmidt's suit pocket following his death.

'And this is my grandfather, Paul Schmidt.'

A bulky, handsome man, he had some kind of gel in his dark hair. I recognised Rosa's own blazing dark eyes, and as he lent forward from a park bench as if to make my acquaintance I thought the likeness was striking.

'So, I will tell you how they met.'

And perhaps because I didn't respond she stopped and looked back over her shoulder. 'It is a famously tragic story in my family but perhaps it is tedious to anyone else.'

'No. No, I want to hear,' I said, and that set her on her way again.

I followed Rosa back to her booth. Her hips gently swayed; it was though she was composing what she would say. She picked up the wine glass next to the adding machine and turned it around in her fingers as though it were an unfathomable object.

'Lionel, be a sweet and fill it up for me, please.'

As I went to take it from her she regarded me over a folded arm, not fondly, but with an exactitude that recalled another similiar time, and said, 'Why don't you have something yourself.'

It had taken more than seven weeks from that first invitation to this second one. And more than a dozen dancing lessons. I took a wine glass from another table and slipped into the booth opposite her.

Rosa leant back. A smoke ring spiralled up to the ceiling while she thought where to begin.

What follows is the story she heard in El Imperio all those years ago. This is the Pacific end of the story. In tango, there are no wrong turns. But every dance begins with a backward step. This is where Louise and Schmidt's story begins, with a backward step.

IN THE LITTLE RIVER CEMETERY, PIG FERN COVERS THE OLDER GRAVES. BUT in one respect, this cemetery is no different from the *cementerio* at Chacarita. The histories of both places are recorded on their tombstones. Story travels along the same branches as genes, and the current inhabitants of Little River are only two beats away from the events of Louise's day.

Of the differences, the key one: death in Little River is a more organic process. The bush inherits everything. Bronzed inscriptions run to an oxidised green. There is not the same vigilance of death that makes La Chacarita the whitewashed splendour it is today.

The grave of Louise's father, James Cunningham, is marked by a river boulder. The inscription reads: 'James Cunningham. Fisherman.

God Bless. Born 1878. Drowned 1911.' Simple. No fuss. That's the way people prefer to sign out in this part of the world.

His boat broke up on the river bar in a storm. Matchsticks and muddy foaming water is what people remember. And that it was another two days before his body turned up. The night slops man saw Jamie Cunningham float on the tide past the dark sleeping houses. He was headed for the mountains, barefoot, with just his trousers on, and a gold wedding band on his finger.

Louise's mother did what widows did in those days and opened her house to boarders and travellers. Two years after they laid the river boulder at her husband's grave she 'succumbed' to the flu and was buried in a grave next to her husband.

People said they hadn't been especially close.

The other headstones in the cemetery record the names of the kids Louise went to school with. These are more 'memory stones'. The graves are empty since the bones of the boys she sat with in class at the Little River School are scattered in fields across Northern France.

In 1915, two years after her mother's death, Louise stood on the road leading out of Little River to watch the boys from her childhood ride out to the war in Europe. They all looked so pleased to be on their way.

Boyd Robertson broke ranks to ride over to her. He bent down from his saddle to receive her kiss.

'Thank you, Louise. I won't forget you,' he said.

When news of Boyd's death came back, Louise liked to think of him reviving that kiss and taking it with him to his last breath. She hoped that when his moment came Boyd gave a sigh of satisfaction as though at the end of a meal and simply closed his eyes.

She saw Royden Jackson searching for some fitting gesture. At the last moment he thought to take off his neck chain and hand it to his mother for safe-keeping. The hell-raising McCracken boys made themselves popular by handing their childhood toys — fishing tackle, a wooden boat on wheels, a teddy bear — to the small boys lining the road out of town. There were others she'd known to cry from a cut knee, or down at the beach to run from the jaws of a shore break with a look of white terror. Boys who believed in the undertow troll and who sweated in their beds at night when the wind in the eaves grew shrill.

Davy McLoughlin's tripod went with him to Europe and returned without him. The attached brown tag read: 'This is the property of . . .' The last Louise saw of him his face was filled with technical considerations to do with light and shadow. He looked like an angel.

She saw the Nial twins ride out side by side. One pale eye each. One corner of a lipless mouth met the other. Limp brown hair held the package together. The face of their mother Audrey appeared flat and spread out.

Everyone worried about the boys. Some more than others. For example, the McCracken boys were given every chance of surviving, even of taking over the world inside six months, while Bunny Sinclair, with his buttoned-up collar and red cheeks, might as well have worn a target on his chest. No one could see how he would get on away from his pigeons.

Boyd was first to be killed. Louise stood in a group of people at the top of the street to see at which house the officer with his envelope of regrets would stop. Seeing it was Hilary Robertson's, Boyd's mother, people breathed out their relief and, silent and remorseful, stared down at the ground in their shame.

A Quaker friend of Louise's, Billy Pohl, was asked to locate Roydon's father in the public bar. He walked up to Jackson and whispered that he had a visitor who wanted a word with him outside. 'Well bring him in here!' boomed Jackson. Billy leant closer to whisper, 'The man is in uniform.' Jackson went quietly after that. By the time he reached the door his face had sectioned off and different parts were trembling. Those he passed on the way to the door either closed their eyes or looked away. Billy stayed back. He thought he'd wait in the bar — though he didn't drink in those days. The publican came out from behind the bar to close the curtains. Everyone braced themselves. Those who heard Jackson's weeping never forgot the 'sound of creaking ruin'.

So these days Louise had company in the cemetery. She would sit by her parents' stone and over there Jackson would crouch by his boy's cross. Audrey Nial would pile blue geraniums between two white crosses. If she had leftovers Louise got those. Mrs McLoughlin was always good for a piece of fruit cake. Often it was Jackson with a bag of sweets; Jackson holding out his white paper bag to Joy or Audrey or whoever else happened to be visiting. That was grief's good side.

It was Billy Pohl who caught her crying at the cemetery one afternoon. Billy told her he wasn't pushing anything at her — but she might think about coming and sitting with his Quakers.

'And do what, Billy?'

'Nothing. You just sit and be quiet.'

Quiet had a roof and it had walls around it, and you could sit inside of it. She had never thought of silence as a place. One of the Friends, Tom Williams, told her, 'The place is in your heart, Louise. Everything else is just clutter.'

By November 1916 there were only two boys of enlistment age left in the district. Billy Pohl and Henry Graham. No one wanted them dead. On the other hand, those who had lost boys were heard to mumble . . . People wondered how the Quakers could pray for those foreign boys that their own boys had gone halfway around the world to shoot. It didn't make much sense when you thought about it — especially to those who had already lost their own.

That might have been the end of it but for a rumour that the recruitment office at Egger's 'cut and shave' was soon to close. All the important news flowed through Egger's — wool prices, coal volumes, marriages, deaths, births, and significantly, which boys had still to sign up.

White feathers were sent Billy and Henry in the mail. People weren't shy about making their thoughts known either and often within earshot. Billy Pohl heard himself described as 'death's guide'. The association wasn't so unreasonable. The first thing the officers did on arriving at the station at Little River with their envelope of condolences was look around for Billy Pohl. Billy was the station guard and knew where everyone in town lived and the shortest route to any house. So when grieving families played back the moment their lives took an unforgettable turn there was the clipped figure in uniform, and there in the background stood Billy Pohl.

On 10 December 1916, Billy Pohl and Henry Graham received letters of official notice that they had been called up. The letter asked them to present themselves at Egger's. Tom Williams went along to speak on their behalf and to explain the 'mix-up'. Billy Pohl and Henry Graham hadn't signed up for anything. Without a word the Recruitment Officer opened his drawer and retrieved two sheets of paper and dragged his finger down to the line with Henry and Billy's forged signatures. The meeting had been reasonably amicable up to now. Tom Williams told the RO, 'You might as well know you can place a rifle in their hands but I can tell you right now they won't shoot.' Royden Jackson's grandfather was in the chair. Two other men as well sat waiting with magazines open in their laps listening to the snip, snip of Egger's scissors. It was perfectly obvious to all what had happened.

Louise came home to find Billy and Henry and Tom Williams in her kitchen. There was an air of gloom. Billy sat chewing his nails. Henry with his head down, scrutinising the floorboards. She did not need to be told the outcome. She boiled some water. She set out some cups and saucers. She poured the tea. Finally, she said, 'I know a place. A hiding place.' There was a cave her father had once pointed out to her. It was five miles outside town. You could stand above it, right over its lip, without knowing what lay beneath you. From the sea it looked like a half-closed mouth; but that was from a moki reef half a mile out. One moment there was the sheer beauty of all that sky and sea and the next you were struck by a devastating loneliness. It was the perfect place for fugitives. Whenever she'd been there with her father the tide drew all the way up to its mouth and cut you off from the world. She was about to talk up its features when Tom Williams cut her off, 'I don't want to hear it, Louise, and it's not because I'm not interested. But should someone ask me where the dickens those boys are you know I won't want to lie.'

They arranged to leave that afternoon. Louise packed away flour and salt, some preservative, three lemons, bagged a number of apples and pulled up some young carrots from the garden. She stuffed everything into the basket strapped to her handlebars together with handy comforts such as old newspapers, soap, the last of the plum tart, and wheeled her bike out to the street.

On the edge of town she stopped to pick some plums from the branch overhanging the fence round the Robertsons' yard. Boyd's mother saw her and put down her washing basket. She said, 'Louise, let me get you a bag for those plums.'

She didn't see another soul until Lion's Rock, and then it was Billy Pohl with his bag and fishing gear. She cycled up to him and told him to walk another two miles, until he found himself at the bluffs, near the nikaus, and to wait there.

She climbed back on her bike and coming up to Jackson's Crossing she saw Henry rise out of the tall roadside grass. Tom Williams was with him. Jackson's was as far as Tom would allow himself to go.

Louise dismounted and stood while the two men shook hands. 'Louise will take you from here, Henry.'

'You'll tell me mum and dad, won'tcha Tom? I don't want them coming after me. Tell them I'm fine and not to worry.'

'I intend to tell them you are in the pink of health and in excellent

55

company.' That wink was for Louise. She smiled. A slow grin showed up on Henry's face.

'In a cave.'

'I didn't hear that, Henry. All I know is that you are going to a safe place.'

'So long as you tell them it's nicer than whatever it really is.' Then he asked, 'What will you tell them, Tom. What, really? I'd like to know.'

Louise watched the older man think for a moment. Henry had just alerted him to a problem he didn't have an answer for yet. He tapped the side of his head — like it was all brilliantly stored upstairs — and placed a hand on Henry's shoulder to point him north. 'Come on, Henry. Louise won't want to be cycling back in the dark.'

They were some distance up the road before Henry said, 'About the dark, Louise. I wouldn't worry. Cycle slow, and steer the front wheel by the breath of the cows. Sometimes you can feel their heat.'

She was so surprised to hear this she stopped wheeling the bike.

'When you think about it, Louise, it's the difference between a stew just cooked and one left to cool a day later.'

She wasn't sure whether Henry had made a joke or whether she had just come into startling new knowledge.

At the bluffs they had a thirty-minute wait until Billy caught up. They listened to the sea pounding on the rocks below and the noise sent Louise's eyes to the long white band on the horizon.

They were sitting on the very edge of the country. This was as far west as one could go.

With her father they had always gone by boat and from the sea you saw a neat line ruled through the nikau trees. The cave, she

56

recalled, was about an inch north of it.

At the nikaus she wheeled her bike in far enough until she was sure it couldn't be seen from the road and laid it down. A green filmy light hung in the treetops. The ground was damp, rich smelling. At first the sound of small twigs snapping marked their progress. But as they walked on the sea grew louder, to where eventually they could smell the salt spray in the trees. After ten more minutes of dark passage under the trees they came out to the great Tasman sky. Huge and blue-lit. Spray rose past their noses from the sea cannoning into the rocks below. They had to shout to hear one another. It was easier to just point the way down to a thin cuticle of white beach. They picked their way down, grabbing and sliding; Billy Pohl with the basket of food. They slid down to the beach and sank up to their thighs in white sea foam.

The next bay was more sheltered. The inshore water was a still, dark jelly bubbling with light and sea necklace. The beach was piled high with kelp torn from the ocean floor; stuck in the craw of its rubbery stalks were stones and small paua. With every footfall black clouds of sandflies flew up at their faces. Billy slapped them away. 'I hope you're sure about where this cave is,' he said. It was the first anyone had spoken in a while and Billy sounded fed up.

She was worried herself that she might not recognise the cave entrance. Four years had gone by since she was last there. Anything could have happened. The entrance might have subsided — the coastline was constantly nibbled away at by the sea. She didn't say anything and they walked on. They walked for another twenty minutes. She was on the brink of admitting to some uncertainty when a cleft in the bank behind the beach caught her eye. 'There,' she said, pointing.

57

A dry creek bed took them inside the mouth of the cave. Its roof lowered and bent away to the left; it turned dark and then light again as they came around the corner to a large area — the size of several rooms. Henry knelt down for a handful of dry sand which he let trickle through his fingers. He gazed up at the pitched roof. Billy looked around at the walls and Louise saw them thinking, 'This isn't so bad.' She watched them poke around, though they did not pay the cave the same close attention as they would have moving into a strange house where every new thing comes in for investigation. They hadn't yet reached the point of thinking about the cave as a place to live. For now, it was just a bivvy to crawl inside until the storm blew over and Tom Williams was able to come to some arrangement whereby they were saved a premature trip to the cemetery.

They left the cave to look north. Beyond the rocks was a long finger of white sand. Higher up the beach lay thickets of driftwood. 'There's your firewood,' Louise said. Henry stared up the beach. He didn't looked so pleased. She watched him turn and gaze back at the cave mouth. His face grew vague, then calculating: 'Louise, do you think if my father was to . . .' She shook her head. Whatever Henry had intended to say he ended himself. 'No, I suppose not,' he said.

An hour later she was pedalling home in the dark, listening out for the soft-breathing cows.

– 8 –

SEVERAL DAYS PASSED BEFORE THE POLICEMAN PAID HER A VISIT. SHE couldn't take her eyes off his acne-scarred face. In his youth the policeman's face had been famously covered in boils.

'Seems we lost two boys, Louise.' He gave the thinnest of smiles as he juggled his notebook and tried to look past her into the hallway.

'That's what I hear, Ryan,' she said.

'There was a thought that you might be of help to our inquiry.'

'Inquire away,' she said. She stepped aside to let him in. He poked his head up the stairwell. His foot was on the first stair when his head gave an unnatural jerk.

'What's that?' he asked.

'A piano.'

59

'Who?' he meant.

'Mr Schmidt. The piano tuner.'

'Schmidt . . .' he repeated after her, experimenting with the sound, the unusual shift it caused in his mouth. He wanted to see for himself.

The lid on the piano was lifted and the piano tuner was sprawled over the piano strings. The backs of his elbows stuck up in the air. Once a year the tuner came and stayed several days and attended to all the pianos up and down the coast. The new man Schmidt was so fully absorbed he didn't notice them standing there. The policeman coughed for his attention and even then the piano tuner was slow to respond. His attention was elsewhere and Louise could see him thinking, whatever the diversion was it could wait a moment. He plucked at the C chord.

The policeman waited; he switched his weight. Finally Schmidt raised his head and Ryan nodded. That was all. He had just wanted to look. He turned to Louise. He said, 'I'll take a peek upstairs if you don't mind.'

She gestured to the stairs.

'After you, Ryan.'

'It's my job,' he said.

Ryan went ahead. She followed close behind. She let him discover on his own which doors led where. There was one awkward moment when he pocketed his notebook and gave a quick look of apology before kneeling to look under the beds.

'You won't find anything there, Ryan,' she said.

'You think this is a joke, Louise. It isn't.'

He looked in the closets, parting racks of coats and dresses. His hand rested on a cotton dress.

She began to laugh.

'There you go again,' he said.

As he came down the stairs, once more the piano tuner's stabbing notes diverted him.

He stopped to ask her, 'How do you spell Schmidt?'

She told him, and he bowed his large head, his lips curling and uncurling as he printed the name. 'Thought so,' he said.

After he left she hurried to the front window where she pulled the curtain back. She saw him out in the street. He was gazing back at the house. He didn't see her though. He bent his head to scribble in his notebook.

Louise wondered what he had seen. She tried to assess the piano tuner through local eyes. She thought his smart clothes set him apart. The cut of his suit. It wasn't the sort of thing you saw much of on the coast. Was he a bit too handsome? Perhaps. Confident? Yes. Look how his face held beneath its surface a glimmer of a smile. The presence of the policeman had amused him. Some might find that patronising. Especially someone who had once found it painful to look in a mirror. She let the curtain go.

She waited a short while, then went into the other room to ask the piano tuner what he fancied for dinner. He looked surprised, happily surprised to have been asked. He glanced over at the clock and it occurred to her that it was a bit early in the day to ask such a question.

'You decide, Louise. I'm sure whatever it is it will be excellent.'

English, she decided then. He's definitely English.

Near the butcher's she became preoccupied by the word 'excellent'. It wasn't a word you heard often. She'd gone and encouraged his anticipation too, now that she thought about it. Never a good thing. A man like the piano tuner, in a suit like his, would have his standards. She pushed through the flyscreen and pointed to a fleshy red steak. She paid more for it than she'd ever paid for Schmidt's predecessor, Angus Wright. Angus Wright used to accept her offer of lamb's fry with a boyish glee. 'Yes, please, Louise.'

Expensive steak warrants new potatoes. She bought a bag and walked home with an empty purse, sick at heart for thinking how poor Billy Pohl and Henry Graham were making do with apples, baby carrots and whatever else they could drag from the sea.

As she turned in the gate she heard the piano. It was her piano, but the music was different from anything she had ever heard. Angus Wright would signal a job well done by rattling off 'Greensleeves'.

Inside the house she put down the groceries and went and stood in the doorway of the front room. The piano tuner looked back over his shoulder and smiled at her. He played on, his shoulders tilting forward as he pressed down on the piano keys. She stayed in the doorway, listening. It was a slow melody. She couldn't place it at all.

Once Schmidt laid his head on his shoulder and tried to coax her over. She thought, oh no. She couldn't. No. No. She tossed her head back and shook it. She laughed. No. Absolutely not. Then the piano stopped.

His face turned serious.

'It is a tango, Louise.'

He watched her to see if anything registered.

Then, 'Here, look. Why don't I show you.'

She moved away from the door. The piano tuner stood up and met her midway across the floor. She moved inside Schmidt's arms. She hadn't danced since school. Boyd had invited her to a big wedding out at one of the farms, and they had danced there, after a fashion. But this was different.

The piano tuner directed her with a series of feints and light shoves. They danced around the room, and then when the song he hummed in her ear showed signs of petering out he would dash back to play a few more bars, rekindle his memory, then return to her with the retrieved melody. Back and forth he went between the piano and her. He played up his forgetfulness and she laughed. They danced and danced until the late afternoon shadows spread over the lawn outside.

At some point, feeling a need for air, they went out to the garden with Louise pulling her cotton shirt away from her clammy skin.

The piano tuner looked well pleased. She remembered her father looking the same way after he had finished building something. He stood with his hands clasped behind his back.

'A drink is what we need, Louise,' he said.

At this hour only Egger's was open. She didn't want to go there. But then she remembered another place that sold lemonade and ice and they set off on foot, leaning into each other, in no hurry. She asked the piano tuner about his travels. It seems he had been everywhere. To France, to Uruguay and to Argentina; to Australia.

'The name Schmidt,' she inquired carefully.

He seemed to know what she was getting at.

'My grandfather was from Bavaria. I was born in Bournemouth.'

She felt herself relax.

They were near the lemonade shop when they heard in the near distance a man shout, 'There he is!'

The voice left a violent arc in the air. They stopped and turned in time to see a figure disappear inside the hotel. The piano tuner gave a shrug. They walked on, though neither one spoke until a little further down the road when they heard something that diverted them. They looked up to see a number of men spill out of the hotel — it was like watching salt poured. Louise saw one with a pick handle. She recognised Jackson; the old fool, she thought, he should know better; and a number of others who were regulars at the Little River Cemetery. The piano tuner fingered his tie. Without any panic, more as though an unexpected change of weather had forced a cancellation of plans, he said, 'I think we might go back now, Louise.'

One of the men shouted, 'You dirty Hun bastard!'

Schmidt looked perplexed. His hand went to his tie again, he placed it on Louise's shoulder to set them on their way.

A number of men had already started across the road. Their intention was obvious. They aimed to cut them off. Louise felt the piano tuner slow at her side. He whispered in her ear, 'The railway station or the police station. Either one.'

The railway station, she thought. It was nearer. Also, the station master might still be there. He had been kind to her; for several months after her father drowned the station master hadn't allowed her to buy a train ticket.

The moment they stopped to alter their course the status of the situation changed. They were quarry now, and awareness of this

64

released new spite and hostility in the shouting that followed them.

They walked faster and faster until Schmidt took her arm and began to run.

They could see the tracks at the end of a long street, but when they arrived there they discovered the station was another two hundred yards away. It was too far. They wouldn't make it. That's when Louise saw the railway jigger.

A year ago, Billy Pohl had taken her for a joyride at night on a jigger. Billy, who had introduced her in to the ways of silence, had wanted to show her the thick comforting silence of the countryside at night. At a certain point Billy had let the lever go and they had rolled through the darkness, the two of them, sitting side by side on the back, trailing their feet, shoulders touching, and Billy quoting to her from the Quaker *Book of Discipline*, George Fox's injunction to 'walk cheerfully over the Earth, ministering to that of God in every person.'

She remembered to release the brake and to raise the arm. She could barely lift it — when she did the front wheels of the jigger creaked slowly forward. The shouting grew louder. Now Schmidt leapt to. Together they worked the lever until they began to build up speed. They were fifty yards north of where they started, and gathering speed, when the mob arrived. Bottles were thrown after them. But none of the mob gave chase. A number of them were railwaymen who knew you couldn't outrun a jigger.

They passed the back yards of houses. Dogs barked from their kennels. And where the tracks came out in farmland a cow burst from the fenceline. The lever was effortless now. There was no resistance whatsoever and Louise was able to do it on her own. Schmidt sat down

65

to rest in a muddle of sweat and confusion. Once the lights of a farmhouse came on and he jumped up to help with the lever. At Jackson's Crossing she pulled on the brake. As they eased to walking pace, she saw Schmidt look warily around at the shadows. She told him not to worry. She knew a place that was safe and where they would never find him.

They tried to push the jigger off the tracks but lacked the strength. So they left it as it was, abandoned between a herd of heifers and sheep. Under early evening skies they crossed a paddock on the seaward side of the tracks. Near the bluffs they heard the gratifying sound of the sea surging in at the rocks. It was pitch black in the nikaus. They had to push ahead of themselves, blindly feeling in the dark for the lighter-built trees. Once when she told him not to worry — just in case he was — that no one would ever find them, she heard him say, 'I can well believe that.'

They came out at a different place to where she had scampered down with Billy Pohl and Henry Graham. In the dark it was rougher going. Schmidt hurt himself, not badly, but enough for him to forget the mob and raise his voice in anger. They crunched along the beach. 'This is ridiculous,' she heard him say. 'I mean, it's not as if I'm German.' And further on, 'I've never been to bloody Germany.' And more irritably, 'Just where the hell are we, Louise?'

She was shocked when she saw the others. Only three days had passed but in the uneven light of the cave Billy Pohl and Henry Graham looked like they had been marooned for weeks. They hadn't shaved. Their faces looked strained. They were relieved to see her though when they saw Schmidt they leapt up. Billy Pohl looked wildly in Schmidt's direction.

66

She began reasonably enough with, 'This is Mr Schmidt, the piano tuner.'

She told them what had happened. Their going out for lemonade. And how the day had suddenly turned on them. Their escape on the jigger pleased Billy especially.

But she also felt their resentment. Where had she been all this time? Why hadn't she brought them food? Henry wanted to know if she had spoken with his parents. What about Tom Williams? Had he given her any news to pass on? Had she remembered to bring tea?

She said, 'I wasn't thinking of tea when we left the house, Henry.'

She walked to the mouth of the cave and stared at the moonlight on the water. Now that they had stopped running she started to notice the night chill. It condensed along her spine. The embers from the fire behind the log in the entrance had died down. She folded her arms and began to think aloud. It was too dark to go back home tonight. She didn't want to climb up the cliff or walk all that way without light.

'Go back?' said Billy Pohl. He sounded amazed. 'You can't go back, Louise. What's the matter with you. They saw you. They saw you with our friend here. 'You go back, Louise, and we might as well walk back with you to our graves.'

- 9 -

She did not know Billy Pohl or Henry Graham that well.
Isolation added to the mystery of the Grahams who lived outside the
town boundary in almost derelict circumstances. A wooden shack
folding into the bush, a solitary square of pasture, the white-freckled
trunks of kahikatea. They were bee-keepers. Also, they didn't eat
meat or so it was rumoured. That was more or less Henry, then. Billy
Pohl she knew as a man of casual habits. Sometimes he would appear
on the brink of growing a beard, then, the next time she saw him
he was shaven, clean as a whistle, the line of his jawbone sporting
and gleaming. With Billy you just never knew what lay around the
corner. It was usually Billy's chair you heard scrape the floor at the
Meetings. Some are able to occupy silence and rug themselves up

in it. Billy was not one of them.

She joined the circle by the fire. Against the cave wall played the flickering shadow of their bowed heads as they sought the comforts of silence. Habits are what you fall back on in a moment of crisis.

She made room for Schmidt but he stuck his hands in his pockets and took himself off to the mouth of the cave to sulk.

That first night, they lay their heads on their folded arms. Sleep came and went. She heard Schmidt get up in the night and move around. She closed her eyes and drifted off again. The next time she woke she raised her head — the mouth of the cave was evenly divided between sky and sea — and she saw him telescoped, sitting on a rock, the moonlit tide washing around him.

Later that morning she was gathering firewood when she heard footsteps in the shingle behind her. She turned, and there he was, holding his hands to her, advancing with an expression of distress. 'I'm sorry, Louise. This is all my fault. I am so sorry.'

Every morning they wake up with the sound of the ocean roaring in their ears. It is the sound of the world in these parts — huge, unpopulated, lonely. They lie there, for the moment too stiff to move, too cold to make the effort even though they know that once they get up and start moving their aches will disappear. They wake with sand in their ears, up nostrils, a grit on their fingers, hands and arms. Skin like sandpaper; their hair stiff. An irritating graininess in their scalp. The itching never stops. Billy Pohl and Henry Graham complain of their filthy trousers; the awful drag of material on their skin is even changing the way they walk. They complain of sores on their legs and soon the discomfort is working its way into their faces, stretching the skin, focussing the eyes, souring mouths.

They raise their heads a few inches and look past their bent knees to the ocean. Another December day lies exhaustingly ahead. By midday Louise is ready to lie down again. She's done everything there is to do. She is ready to lie down and sleep. By midday she finds herself wishing for nightfall. The afternoon is no use to her. There is nothing to do but to wait.

Meanwhile the hills, the tireless ocean, the broad sky all carry the same message. Look at where you are. You're all alone.

At night when the wind blows down off the hills they lie in their sand beds with the thought that they are as powerless as the cows that stand in their dark paddocks. As vulnerable as the land peaking out to sea. Anything could happen. An earthquake. A giant wave might engorge the cave and suck them out to join the echo of the ocean and of nothingness.

By the fourth day it is clear to Louise that things are not going to pan out the way she thought they would. The world hasn't missed them at all. The world isn't even out searching. Either that, or they've done too good a job of hiding and now they are left with just themselves. Louise in her fraying dress. Paul Schmidt with that secret country he carries within. Self-sufficient and the least ruffled of them, always he seems locked in his thoughts, travelling between the here and there. Billy, cat smart, watchful. And Henry, glum, bored with the adventure, like a child in his persistence, asking every hour, why hasn't Tom come for them? Why hasn't Tom brought the good news that he's sorted out things and they are now free to return to their other life?

Why have they been left to hang here like this?

The same question preoccupies them all. Billy is given to standing in the mouth of the cave where he quizzes the sea.

Schmidt has made a particular rock his own. He can spend hours sitting on it, alone, knees, chin and elbows. The moment he senses anyone's eyes on him he returns their interest with a smile. Louise hasn't heard him complain once — even in the morning he never joins in the chorus of groans. She watches him sitting on his rock and thinks, he is like a man waiting for a late-arriving train.

Most days a trawler is seen out to sea. A single vee slicing a line for farther up the coast. It is always Billy who hisses at her to get down from the rock. Billy is always on the lookout. Every morning he climbs the cliff behind the cave to check their position in case in the night there has occurred some re-arrangement. Billy is the one most suspicious of the world. She doesn't get down from the rock, though. She doesn't believe that the trawler has seen them. She's convinced of their invisibility. Besides, she's been out on her father's boat and knows about the bulge in the sea and how the shoreline disappears from view.

One night Schmidt tells a story about South American animals with magical powers who at night turn themselves into ghosts and sneak into villages, passing through the front door of houses, searching the shelves for food.

In the ensuing silence it is Billy Pohl who speaks up. 'We're not about to do that,' he says.

Of the unmentionable things, of all the things she is sure preoccupies

71

Billy, it is this. What if Henry bolts? What if one morning they wake up and find him gone? That would be it then, wouldn't it? That would mean the end. It would only be a matter of time before a sheepish-looking Henry led the authorities to their whereabouts.

The prospect made her smile. A sense of relief loosened within her; for the moment it was as if Henry had already gone and done that and now there was just a short period of waiting to get through before the dogs and handlers showed up. She looked over at Paul Schmidt sitting on the rock, crossed arms, locked in a dream. They would let him go, and he would say adieu. To where? Abroad? He wouldn't stay a piano tuner. Or if he did, it wouldn't be here. Europe? Not with all the fighting. He would go to Argentina. He would go to that place he describes at night around the fire. He would go there and lose himself in a new language. She thinks how wonderful that would be, to simply leave and arrive, and in time become local. It makes her feel a little sad, even envious. And what about Henry and Billy? What would happen to them? Well, that's easy, isn't it. They would be marched off to the war to be killed out of fairness to old classmates.

The thought made her groan out loud. Immediately the others looked at her.

She smiled, shook her head. Said it was nothing.

She opened the palms of her hands to release the thoughts.

'See? All gone.'

Boredom. What to do. What to do. How to fill the hours. She wishes someone would find them. She wishes it would pass. It's Saturday and she wants to go to the cemetery. Is it even Saturday? It feels like it might be. She can't be sure. She's lost all track of time.

They live as prisoners experience life. Without a sustaining present. Without even a future to grasp hold of. So they talk about the past. Billy tells stories. Henry tries to. He never seems sure whether or not he has embarked on a story. He will begin talking, then look at each of their faces — unsure in which direction to direct the flow of information. He speaks of events, incidents from the farm. Or of things with a scientific bent. How bees carry honey under their wings and the miraculous creation of the honeycomb. Henry can look at a piece of honeycomb and tell exactly where, and from which flower, the bees have been gathering. But more often it's the piano tuner they turn to. He speaks of a place that sets their dreaming selves loose. Of crazy bars where the white people copy the black people, and dance with all their innermost self and feeling, where one dancer follows another, and one dance follows another, hour after hour, until the night peels back to dawn.

One night the piano tuner unfolds himself from his place by the fire. He shakes the sand off his trousers and snaps his fingers for Louise to get up and join him. So that they can see for themselves what he's been talking about, he will show them a few steps of the tango.

Before the fire-lit faces of Billy Pohl and Henry Graham she feels the piano tuner's hand arrive at the small of her back. The hand gives a little shove and resettles. It presses and guides; Schmidt hums; it is the same music she's heard him play in her front room. She laughs — but that is more for Billy Pohl and Henry Graham's sakes, to make them relax. The piano tuner's eyes are still, concentrated — now they move

73

off. They prospect in one direction, then shift their weight there. They do not hurry. She likes that. The way he moves her with exaggerated slowness. And because it is dark she is able to close her eyes and float in his arms, and smile at the flow of instruction to Billy Pohl and Henry Graham. 'You see? Yes? Yes?' For a second they hold the position — hold it, hold it. 'You see, yes?' until the shiny faces by the fire nod back.

Billy Pohl has a turn. Then Henry Graham. Billy holds her too tightly. He doesn't want to so much guide her as possess her, clamp her on to himself and run off with her. With Henry it is like she might crumble into a thousand pieces.

'Henry,' she whispers. 'I can't feel your hand.'

She can hear his tremulous breath though.

'Go on, Henry, don't be shy.'

But her back is a hot coal and Henry can't keep his hand there for long.

The piano tuner sings. He sang in Spanish. Words that none of them can understand. It is the only tango song Paul Schmidt knows in its entirety so he sings it repeatedly until they get to know the words and at a certain bend in the song are able to join in.

When she dances with Henry the piano tuner fits the song around Henry's uncertainty. He slows it down. He even stops it to instruct Henry on some point. With Billy the song tends to speed up; it is a race to the finish and that is Billy's fault. He tries to fit in more turns than necessary. Sometimes Louise thinks she catches a glimpse of the finish tape in Billy's eyes.

The sand on the floor of the cave is quick to cut up. After each dance they move to another area of the cave until that too cuts up, and then they begin over, Paul Schmidt singing, one or the other of the boys clapping to keep the rhythm.

Morning finds the floor of the cave churned up. It looks like a herd of cattle has passed through.

It was Billy Pohl who 'discovered' the dance floor. An area of flat rock on one side of the cave. It sloped away but other than that it behaved fine. After Billy brushed away the sand they watched Schmidt measure it out in steps. Four to the side, ten to the end where he stopped to scratch his chin and ponder. 'Louise?' He looked around for her and held out a beckoning hand. She moved inside his arms. He whispered the instructions and they demonstrated the *gancha* — a thigh glance inviting an upward flick of her heel inside his leg that brought a 'Holy Jesus' from Billy looking on. 'You see,' said the piano tuner calmly. 'There doesn't have to be a lot of movement to make it interesting.'

They were learning in their different ways. Billy Pohl had a turn; then Henry. But it was Schmidt whom Louise waited for. Billy and Henry were just something to get through. They liked the womanly feel of her. They liked to feel her close, Billy especially, he became like a vine, clamping on to her; Henry, on the other hand, wanting to but not quite able to and going slack with shame. She danced longer with Schmidt. For one thing, the piano tuner could carry the song and add as many verses as he wished. He could hum in her ear. Not only was he the master of technique he was in charge of music, which gave him a distinct advantage over Billy Pohl and Henry Graham. In their hands the dance was a clumsy, awkward thing. Whereas it flowed out of Schmidt. Well, it was in him to start with. Bit by bit Louise found herself stowing bits of the dance inside of herself, the sandwich, for example, and when the piano tuner dragged her foot back with his own she felt a glass chandelier must be hanging over them, a band playing onstage, floorboards gleaming in the lights.

– 10 –

AT LOW TIDE THE WORLD RECONFIGURED. THE SEA DREW BACK AND THE
tide turned lazy with sloppy brown kelp beds. Rocks emerged, and
seabirds found new quarters to rest on and watch the day.

Louise was sitting on a rock watching Billy Pohl show the piano
tuner how to reach down and feel for paua. Both men were in their
long johns, Schmidt with the side of his face flat to the water; his eyes
squeezed tight with concentrated effort. She thought of him tuning the
piano, feeling for the notes.

It was the same when they danced together. She watched his eyes.
They coaxed her, assisted by his shoves and tips; and his quiet words of
encouragement. 'Good, Louise. That's it. You've got it.' When his mouth
closed a line ran from the corner to halfway up his cheek. Once they

were safely through the step or series of steps the lines of his jaw would soften again. She was picking it up. Her progress seemed to please Schmidt as much as it did her. He told her, 'You can dance, Louise. You can do it.'

Once, while gathering firewood, she felt sufficiently light and confident enough to ask him, 'Are you married, Mister Schmidt?' Falling back on formality in a jokey way.

'No,' he said. 'Are you?'

'No,' she said.

They left it at that.

These days it was too hot to linger. The sun hogged the sky and scorched the grey beach, making it too hot to walk barefoot on. During the hottest part of the day they holed up in the cave, huddling in the highest corners to protect their red bitten shins from the sandhoppers and sandflies.

There were duties to perform. Small tasks that in themselves were diverting. In the next bay there was water to collect from a hill stream where they would drop to their knees and dip their faces and drink as the cattle did. Separately they took themselves off to the creek to strip off their rags and soak them.

They went swimming, Billy Pohl and Henry Graham several times a day, Schmidt not so often. He was just as happy with his rock where he could sit alone and think.

To get a moment by herself, or to bathe, Louise would walk all the way to the end of the beach where a finger of rock pushed out to sea like a breakwater. Inside it were a number of rocks and rock pools to choose from. Billy Pohl and Henry Graham entered the sea in their long johns. But she could not bear the way her dress stiffened with the saltwater once it dried, so she went in naked.

There were days when the wind blew up and flung spit across the beach. Summer squalls that sent them running for the cave. Then the wind would stop dead and the head of a dandelion would come to a complete rest on the beach. It was as though the weather had stopped to pause and think, 'What now?' before deciding it might as well rain. And rain it did. Inside the cave they looked out at the tiny waterfalls cascading over the entrance. Out to sea heavy grey lines like guy ropes held the sky in place. And when the rain stopped and the sun came out they left the cave to find jets of fresh water spurting out of the limestone bluffs above the beach. Some of these fell thirty feet and they ran to stand under them, squealing with pleasure and gasping at the cold.

After three days the waterfalls slowed to a trickle. They made wet streaks against the rock face. Then just a line of mist as the last of the waterfall evaporated. Finally, nothing. Or at least it returned to bare rock face. And at dusk they could lean against the limestone and feel the warmth of the day where, just a few days earlier, it had spurted with water.

For a spell it was stifling hot and none of them had the energy to climb up to the hill creek for water or to wash. The fatigue Louise felt had nothing to do with the dancing at night. It was dehydration. The light headacheyness. The sandbagged weariness. The effort it took just to drag herself up the beach. They weren't drinking enough water. She knew that. But immersion in the sea momentarily revived her; then she felt her body solidify and gather its old self. Now she slid up on to a rock, found a place to sit. With her fingers she brushed her wet hair back from her face. The salt cleared from her eyes and when she looked to the beach there was the piano tuner. Something inside her gave a start. On the surface though she was perfectly calm. He nodded to her. She did the same. Then he turned and walked back down the beach.

They danced again that night. She danced with Henry first, then Billy. The piano tuner got the song going. In the light of the fire Schmidt approached her with a smile. 'Louise.' When he spoke her name she had an idea he was thinking of her as he had seen her that morning, naked, and drying herself on the rock.

One night they failed to notice the 'music' stop, and continued to rock back and forth in each other's arms, a slow, rhythmic motion. It was as though she was floating — a liquid kind of contentment. Then all too suddenly she was aware of a change. She felt Schmidt's hand leave her back. She lifted her face off his chest, and the two of them looked over at the fire. The pair of boiling eyes belonged to Billy Pohl. The slack face was Henry's, injury and perhaps awe combined there.

She felt Schmidt move to distance himself. A shift in his attention. And in a bid to focus on Billy and Henry he cleared his throat. 'Do you see what I mean now. You only need minimal movement to make it interesting. Minimal movement.'

Henry found a twig to divert himself. Billy dropped his gaze.

'Billy, you want to try?'

Billy looked up; his eyes burned a trail through the shadows to Louise. 'Nope,' he said.

80

Now Louise joined in. She said, 'Come on, Billy. Please. Pretty please.'

'Henry,' asked Schmidt. 'How about you?'

Henry stole a quick look at Billy and shook his head.

Henry was the easier of the two to pick on.

Schmidt placed his hands on his hips and tried to look amused.

'Henry, I'm surprised at you. You don't stand a lady up.'

Henry rubbed his shoulder.

'I've got sunburn,' he said.

That night Louise lay down in a special sand bed that Henry had lovingly made for her earlier in the day; it was raised and covered with flax, and almost comfortable. She could have kissed him and it would have felt the most natural thing in the world but she pulled back with the thought that then she would have to kiss them all evenly and fairly. And what was an innocent impulse would be turned in to something else like 'an equal share', and such an arrangement would seem too much like commerce.

– 11 –

BY LOUISE'S ESTIMATION THEY HAD BEEN LIVING IN THE CAVE FOR MORE than three weeks when another being came into their lives.

She saw him after swimming one morning. She had climbed over the point for the view south. And there he was. She'd forgotten what other people looked like. He was a heavily built man with white and brown rippling folds of flesh. The water rippled too. It rippled against that part of his torso that rose out of the water to a wide back, round shoulders and two club-like arms. Had he looked up and turned his head he would have seen her. Yet she felt there was almost no chance of him doing that. All his attention was concentrated on the minute task of peeling black shellfish off the rocks. It was like watching someone search for nits in another's scalp. The rest of the world didn't concern him.

She climbed back down to the beach where she dressed and hurried back to the cave with her news. She had seen someone. Aside from the lights of the fishing boats they saw at night the shellfish gatherer was the first visitor they'd had from the world they'd abandoned. Now she had another thought and this one slowed her. What if the man was to make his way into their bay? That he would seemed inevitable. In the short time she watched him he had progressed from rock to rock in her direction. Now a different thought occurred to her. What about Henry? What if she told them of the visitor, and Henry took the opportunity to slip away? How long before the rest of them were rounded up, and then what? There would be no more dancing lessons. That was the first thing. Secondly, Schmidt would disappear from her life. His firm hand would slide from her back forever. His soft brown eyes would turn away, never to look back. There would be no more exotic stories of impoverished songwriters who walked the streets selling their lyrics or of animals ghosting their way into houses at night, or accounts of lives that had changed in the course of a single dance. Thirdly, her life would stop changing. She would go back to the old one. The old routine of taking in boarders and travellers and of visiting the cemetery on Saturdays. She thought of Jackson with his white paper bag of sweets. She thought of her parents and they seemed more dead than they ever had before. Dead, and unreclaimable. By the time she reached the cave she'd made up her mind. She wouldn't say anything to the others. For now, at least, the shellfish gatherer would be her secret.

They danced that night.

Schmidt introduced Billy Pohl and Henry Graham to the rocking step that had so scandalised them a few nights earlier. She could feel Billy pulling her into him. Henry just leant against her. She noticed Schmidt give himself completely over to the others. He crouched like a blacksmith shoeing a horse to correct the position of errant feet. He encouraged Henry to step more inside the embrace. Billy he got to extend his front leg so she could flick her bare ankle up; and when she did so, her calf brushing his, she saw Billy smile, as if at a pleasurable taste in his upper palate. On top of this instruction Schmidt kept the song going. He was there strictly for the benefit of the others. Very deliberately, Louise felt him avoid her eye. She didn't get to dance with him at all.

By the time they lay down by the embers of the fire to sleep she felt the evening had been wasted. The sea made its listless noises. It slurped and drew back around the rocks. It was a full moon, and there was enough light for her to see a crab crab-walk into the cave entrance. There, it stopped to look around before moving on to search for lodgings farther up the beach. She managed to smile. She realised she had become used to the cave. It wasn't so bad. On the surface at least it had grown to be tolerable. In other more vital ways, she had never felt more alive. She just wished she had got to dance with the piano tuner. She *needed* to dance with him. And what a shift that represented. Who'd have thought three weeks ago when she packed up provisions that dance might be more important to her than water?

Far out to sea she saw a shooting star grow bright, turn brighter, then die in a burst of incandescence. There went her old life. She heaved a sigh and returned to listening to the sleeping breath of Billy Pohl and Henry Graham. She thought of the shellfish gatherer. Then, tired of these thoughts, tired of thinking and of being awake, she switched herself on to her side to find Schmidt awake beside her. She saw him smile. In the half light he looked like a jowly lion. He must have been looking at her all this while. Now he marched his fingers across the sand and spread his hand over hers. He kneaded each finger. Circled her palm with his forefinger. Caressed. Probed. She closed her eyes and let his fingers explore her neck and cheek. There was a sudden noise, a shuffle of rearrangement from one of the others, and his hand withdrew in to darkness.

In the morning, on her way back from the hill stream, she climbed the point. Her hair was still wet, and a cooler sea breeze than usual goosepimpled her skin. The wind was from a different quarter. The shellfish gatherer was back, his heavy shoulders digging in the sea. She was shocked by his progress. She had imagined him going from one rock to the next, progressively, more or less in order. She hadn't expect him to be so random about it. But there in the sand was the drag of his sack where he had walked along the beach in search of an entry point into the sea.

She climbed down and ran back along the beach. She met Schmidt sitting on a log a short distance from the cave. He stood up in his leisurely, bemused way.

'Where are the others?' she asked him.

He shrugged and pointed vaguely.

'Henry's gathering firewood. I don't know where Billy is. Up at the stream?'

'Then we can dance,' she said.

He was slow to take her words on board. Or perhaps that was just a ploy while he thought of a way to turn down the invitation?

'Just us,' she said, in case he had other thoughts.

The piano tuner's smile faded. He looked behind.

'No one will know,' she said.

'One dance.' She saw him calculating the quantity of danger 'one dance' represented. He started to nod his head.

'Just the one,' he made her promise.

'One is good,' she said, knowing that one dance could be for a long, long time.

As they hurried to the cave Schmidt tried to get her to see it from his point of view. It was a 'delicate situation'. It wasn't that he didn't want to dance.

'Please understand that,' he said. He raised his shirtsleeve to adjust a cufflink that had long ago disappeared. She told him to relax. It was just a dance for goodness sakes. But she smiled as she said this. It was an insincere voice, one that adults use for children. She was as excited as Schmidt. Still, she told him he was worrying over nothing.

'Not over nothing Louise,' he said.

She didn't think he was going to say it, admit it out in the open. But he did.

'You know what Billy's like,' he said.

She noticed his forehead. It was sweating. And when he took hold of her his hands were clammy.

'Plus,' she said, just in case he had other ideas, 'I want to hear you sing.'

They danced, after a fashion. They danced in spite of themselves. Louise couldn't stop herself thinking of the shellfish gatherer, the threat he posed. Just as a new life was taking shape for her, too. Schmidt, on the other hand, trained his attention on the cave entrance. There was a male wariness about him. He sang, though very softly and without much conviction, until finally the words drifted away entirely and when he began to hum she told him, 'No, I want to hear the words.'

At a certain point though the song ended and Schmidt stopped and released her. He stepped back and held his hands away from her. 'One dance. I thought we agreed.'

This was one of the times she could have told him about the shellfish gatherer. He wouldn't be so cautious if he knew their days might be numbered. On the other hand she couldn't be sure of his reaction. He was a hard one to judge. He might turn out to be like Henry. Given half a chance she was sure Henry would conspire to let himself be seen. Probably he would just turn himself in; like the man who chooses to fall from a cliff face rather than persist with the mental agony of hanging on. Wishing for certainty above all else.

She could give up the cave. She could give it up at a moment's notice. The cave was just part of the fit. The shell enclosed about the succulent bit. But she couldn't give up Schmidt. She would have to get rid of the shellfish gatherer.

She had run through the scene many times. In her own mind, when she approached the stranger he would look up and she would bide her time, like God with all the answers, or a train conductor on his approach along the carriage, or the grocer, neat dapper Mr Fawls

87

who her father had approached for credit one time during a poor fishing season.

It could have been for as long as a minute that she stood at the edge of the tide waiting to be 'discovered'. She watched the shellfish gatherer with his blind man's movement; saw his thick shoulders hover and bob. When at last he sensed he had company his head appeared to snap back. The sea let go of his white singlet and poured off his huge stomach. The rest was the unrehearsed part.

The man's face reported back what he saw. A woman fallen out of the sky. Her bare feet, the sun-faded and torn black dress. His eyes ran over her, noting detail. His silent examination caused her to raise a hand to her uncombed hair.

He may have said something at that moment. The shape of his mouth suggested 'What?' That may have been the end or the start of what he said. A wave flopped noisily ashore and spilled a million glass fragments.

She raised her dress over her thin legs as far as her waist. She invited the shellfish gatherer to look, which is what he did. He did look. Though only briefly, because he looked up again as if to check with her.

She meant to say, *You can touch.* To make it easier on both parties she cast her eyes out to sea. She took on the forbearance of the hills that take no notice of events at their feet, and waited for the man to drag himself from the water. He hauled his sack and dumped it on the wet sand. Louise thought she saw the red shell of a crab crawl out the opening. He let go of the sack, and with the hand he'd used to pick up shellfish he reached towards her as if to pick up something off a shelf; that's when she took a well-rehearsed step back.

He was unshaven. Dark around the eyes. A rough-shaped mouth.

'I know who you are,' he said. 'You're that woman.' As he said that he looked back at the point separating the two beaches.

'They're gone,' she said quickly. 'They went north a week ago.'

He kept gazing up at the skyline above the point. She didn't think any of the others would show themselves. She'd made a point of telling Henry in passing that she was going to the hill stream. The man lost interest in the sky. The revelatory moment he had hoped for failed to reveal itself. She saw him reconsider. He set his teeth against his bottom lip and looked back at her. Then he dropped his eyes to what her raised dress revealed. A puzzled but interested look took hold of his face. He made a move towards her and once again Louise quickly stepped back, though still with her skirts riding around her hips.

'First promise me something.'

She waited until the man nodded.

'Promise me you won't ever come back here again.'

He nodded.

'And that you won't tell another living soul.'

Again he nodded.

'What?' she said.

'Right,' he said this time.

'Because if you do people will find out about this.'

The man's face whitened. She thought perhaps she shouldn't have said that. She didn't want to scare him away.

'One touch is all you get,' she said.

The hand that tore shellfish from the rocks was laid against her. Thinking it would be unpleasant she looked away and found a

89

slow-moving cloud to focus on. But it wasn't quite as she had thought it would be. It wasn't unpleasant. It was no more and no less than interesting. The shellfish gatherer kept his hand there. Loyal to the task. She heard him sigh and it was like the breath of a man grown tired of waiting. Or simply wanting to move on to the next thing. It occurred to her that time was up. She let go of her dress and reluctantly, the shellfish gatherer withdrew his hand under the falling curtain of fabric.

'Don't forget,' she said.

The shellfish gatherer looked down at the wet sack. It moved and crawled with sea life. He looked back at the sea. She saw him frown. It had just dawned on him what he had agreed to give up.

How easy it was. Every unrehearsed moment falling in to place. Everything with its own pulse shifting with tidal inevitability. He'd coughed a lot: that was really the worst of it. Coughed again as he touched her. She didn't feel bad or guilty as she had thought she would. She didn't think or feel much other than a curiosity — and this, which was the surprising part, a continued light pressure where the shellfish gatherer's hand had been.

The feeling stayed with her, that light pressure. She worried that it would pull certain strings in her face. The world had its ways of leaking information. She remembered as children, how careful they had been to brush away the crumbs of the pinched biscuits.

The panic of the past few days lifted and Louise returned to the daydream of chores and division of labour. There was firewood to collect. 'Beds' to be made. Paua to scrape off the ocean bed, its flesh to wrap in cloth and beat to a pulp then slice and cook on the skillet. There was the usual talk on whether or not the world had forgotten them. More speculation as to what had happened to Tom Williams. That was a concern. She also mentioned to the others that they were running out of salt. But no one said anything, preoccupied as they were with the one thing. The resolution of 'the situation'.

Billy and Henry repeatedly told one another Tom would come when he thought it was safe. They must have been watching him otherwise Tom would have come for them by now, for sure. Leave it to Tom to figure out a way. Tom will outsmart them. Hell, everyone knew Tom could look you in the eye and make the hills move without you knowing.

These discussions didn't include Schmidt. He didn't know this Tom Williams, or his saintly power, and so removed himself to the mouth of the cave to stare at the horizon and watch another day depart, another night fall.

At night, with the flames crackling at his back, the piano tuner turned away. It was a private moment that she both wondered about and resented him for. She was sure that Schmidt's thoughts wheeled and circled in a place richer than her own. And because that place did not include her — how could it? — she envied the piano tuner these moments alone. This entry into his other life. Or his next. The one that would exclude her. Whereas she had only this one to ponder and contemplate. This one life because it was richer than any she had known. She stared at the piano tuner's back with these mixed feelings. And while it was also true that if you stared long enough at the horizon eventually your eyes burned a space big enough to call your own,

Schmidt wasn't allowed to idle there for long.

The eager hand clapping of Billy Pohl and Henry Graham snapped the piano tuner back to the here and now, this sandy, sticky, sandfly-plagued cave. Billy and Henry's efforts at managing the tango beat pulled him out of that space he had cleared for himself. From a crosslegged position, they leant forward slapping their hands and howled the few remembered Spanish words he'd taught them. And the piano tuner, appreciative, though with just a bit of hangdog capitulation pulling on the edges of his smile, came gliding back inside the cave. He smiled at Louise and raised his arms; and she smiled back, shifting her shoulders a bit this way and that. She moved inside his arms as she had on numerous other occasions. The piano tuner shifted his left leg forward which was a signal for her to move hers back. But at that same moment he forestalled her. She felt him exert pressure on her back. He dropped his head and she rose to meet his lips. They hadn't rehearsed that before. On the other hand, it didn't feel like something they might get wrong. She tasted his mouth, his rough whiskered lips. That was all they had time for because the 'music' stopped.

It was silent. A piece of dried sea necklace popped in the fire. She felt Schmidt release her. His mouth. Then his hand on her elbow. Bit by bit she was being released.

Billy stood up, his world turned upside down before his eyes. Louise once saw a man arrive home to his house on fire. Billy had that same look of loss and bewilderment. Henry sat on the floor of the cave, his head down, drawing the sand up and letting it go between his fingers.

Somebody needed to say something. Schmidt chose to. He stepped away from her and he spoke in Billy's direction.

'You could let me go. I'll walk north and pick up a ride over the pass. No one would find me. I'd be gone from your lives.'

There it was. Neat. Tidy. That other world beckoning.

Schmidt went on, 'No one would track me back to here. I'd be gone. Out of your lives.'

Billy Pohl turned away to the mouth of the cave and looked out.

Schmidt continued. 'You don't need me here, Billy. You know they aren't looking to sign me up.'

Billy Pohl picked up a stone and flung it at the sea.

Henry had dropped his chin on to his chest. Now he looked up and caught Louise's eye. He nodded for her to join him outside. That's right, it would be dark soon, and there was still firewood to collect. Any excuse would do. She needed to do something.

She moved quickly by Schmidt.

'Louise,' she heard him say. She knew he would want to explain. But she kept moving. It was Henry's hand she felt on her shoulder propelling her on.

Tom Williams always said false words were a sin. So Henry didn't say anything at all and she was glad of that. They walked up the beach, the shingle giving under their feet. 'Henry,' she said, and when he stopped to hear what she meant to say she said, 'Nothing. It's nothing.' She had been on the brink of telling him about the shellfish gatherer. She just wanted to tell him something for the sake of saying something new. Perhaps she wanted to show that she could surprise the world as well. More likely it was grief at the sacrifice she'd made and the collapse of the wildly romantic hopes she'd nourished, wishing to make themselves heard. She wanted someone to know about this. She wanted compensation.

They started to collect firewood. She was glad to have this to do. Though when she bent down for the first piece the tears inside her had just been waiting for such a slope to run down. Henry must have heard her because he let go of the driftwood in his arms. She heard his loyal responsive steps in the shingle. She sniffed back the tears. She said, 'I haven't cried like this since . . . Since . . .' She didn't know when. She was going to say since her mother's funeral. But that wasn't right; not exactly. On that occasion she had felt less sorry for herself than she did for her mother and the hollowness that she'd clasped following her father's drowning. She hadn't known how to live without her husband. That was the first realisation. The second — she realised she didn't want to. Now Henry held out a hand to her as if to say she could have that if she wished, if she had a use for it. He told her everything would be all right. Then he offered the only thing he knew that worked for him. 'Tom'll come for us when he thinks the time is right.'

Soon they had gathered enough driftwood. They were on their way back when Billy Pohl came out to help. Henry told him they had enough for the night and although Billy nodded that he'd heard and understood, he went on picking up stray bits here and there.

At the mouth of the cave Schmidt tried to make eye contact with her. He took his hands out of his pockets to take firewood from her, but she turned her shoulders away. She didn't need help. But she didn't want his in particular.

She didn't speak to the piano tuner again. That night she lay with her back to him, and when she woke up in the morning he was gone.

In the sand next to where he slept, he had written with a stick, 'Bye Louise, I shan't forget you.' There was a squiggle after 'you'. She thought it might be a kiss. She looked at it from another angle. It was a kiss. She glanced over at the sleeping figures of Billy Pohl and Henry Graham. There were no messages for them so she smoothed out this one left for her.

For the next day or two no one remarked on Schmidt's departure. It was too hotly contested by other thoughts. Too hot a subject to handle in their tender state. They skirted mention of him by plunging into silence and living like phantoms. They slept, and woke to chores that they no longer had any heart for. Louise dragged herself to the stream to drink and wash. It took such an effort to walk up the beach, to pick each foot out of the shingle, that she wondered if she was ailing. She had lost weight. They all had. She hungered for something sweet to eat. Anything other than the black leathery paua flesh. An apple would be nice. A glass of cool milk. Henry Graham smacked his lips in his sleep. They all salivated in their dreams. And long after she swallowed them down, the bits of paua sat individually and rejectedly in the pit of her stomach. Even her intestinal juices had tired of the monotony. She forced herself to sit up straighter, to snap out of this food obsession. And while physical discomfort could be admitted, owned up to and wilfully dismissed, banishing the piano tuner from her thoughts was a much harder task. Schmidt had taken up residence in that part of her over which she had less control.

Left alone and at night clutching herself in her sand bed she thought about the kiss from Schmidt. What if Henry Graham and Billy Pohl hadn't been there? What if the kiss had been taken at a more private moment? Had the incident been premeditated or had the piano tuner simply taken his opportunity as he had the kiss? He had been so quick to speak up. A bit too quick to make his case to Billy. She wondered where he was now. She placed him on a dark road walking by the moonlight. She heard him singing to himself and hated him all the more.

Yet it was Louise who made the effort to get them dancing again. It would be good for their morale, she thought. One night she walked over to the dance floor. Henry rolled away from her invitation. He lay back dreaming up at the cave ceiling. So she called over to Billy, 'Will you dance with me, Billy?' She saw him give it a thought. He wanted to. He took his hands out of his pockets, managed a step towards her, then changed his mind. Without a word said he turned and walked out of the cave. She had an idea that he wanted to her to follow him. Instead, she went and lay down to wait for morning.

It was this waiting that got to them in the end, and the following day when Henry Graham proposed that he might walk south and look for a sign of Tom Williams, there was no objection from her or Billy Pohl. They were so tired of waiting to be found.

– 12 –

BILLY POHL NOW SLEPT WHERE SCHMIDT HAD BEEN, OCCUPYING THE SAME hollow in the sand, and Louise slept with her back to Billy to prevent him mapping her thoughts as they came and went on her face. Everything was easier in the dark. You could think one thing and say another.

In the dark Henry was able to opine, 'If they catch him it will be curtains for us.'

'*If* they catch him, Henry.' She allowed herself that because to stay quiet was almost as bad as saying too much.

'So, Louise.' It was Billy now, prefacing his next thought with a calculated pause. 'Where would you say he's headed?'

'England. South America. I really don't know, Billy.' She meant to sound vague.

It was the first time they'd mentioned Schmidt since he left them.

One night Billy Pohl got up from the fire and wandered circumspectly over to the dance floor. She watched him, hands in pockets, kick away the sand and rake the small stones clear with his bare foot. Then he looked across his shoulder for her and held out a hand.

There wasn't much in the way of music. The singular handclaps of Henry which sounded like half-hearted attempts to slap a bothersome sandfly. Billy held her firmly. He hardly moved at all. She felt his rough face against hers. His urgent whisper, 'Show me how, Louise. Show me how to do it.' So she tried to show him. She talked him through the steps. 'Back. Across. Now, forward. That's it, Billy.' But he couldn't do it. His legs got tied up, and in his frustration he pushed her away and shook his head. She told him they could try again in the morning. And Billy nodded, 'In the morning then.'

They did not dance again.

It was January, they realised, by the number of longliners out at sea. They tried calculating back to pinpoint Christmas. In the course of their routine nothing they ever did cut very deeply into any one day to make it memorable. The weeks fell away to a blur. The more vivid moments that came back to Louise involved the piano tuner — his brazen stare at her sunbathing naked on the rock, the playful march of his fingers around her neck, the gauge of feeling a quick glance allowed when the backs of the others were turned, the way he said her name, and above all, their dancing. There was also the shellfish gatherer's uneven breath, his torn shorts, the pressure he lightly applied. That came and went along with the moment she and Schmidt kissed, and that other moment when she had felt life itself spill out of her on waking up to find the piano tuner gone. These of course were deeply personal memories. Time as a public record was less spectacular, a sameness that failed to cut up the days into neat and memorable portions.

By now the limestone bluffs had completely dried up. It was hard to believe that water had ever poured out of them. Even the sea had stopped shifting about, as if it too were conscious of sparing itself extra effort. The heat turned sticky. They became listless. Just to trudge across the piping hot sand and up the hill to the creek required supreme effort. And when they got there they found the creek water was low and brackish. It was easier to stay in the cool of the cave and gaze out at the world and wonder why it had left them to rot.

One night she woke with a fierce headache. She'd had them before but this headache was different. The ache seemed to float and shift in a bubble inside her skull. The only relief was when she turned from one side to the other, but it was fleeting, the pain briefly put aside, and for her trouble when it returned it was worse than before, expanding until her skull was fit to burst. Billy knelt by her, massaging her head. He pulled gently on the ends of her hair. For a brief time this led the throbbing away. Then she grew faint.

She heard Billy and Henry discussing her. She heard Henry say: 'She's dehydrated. She needs water.' After a pause, she heard Billy answer. 'All right,' he said. 'I'll go.' He sounded tired. Then she heard them scratching around for the saucepan. Beyond her closed eyelids she heard Billy swear, then she must have passed out. The next thing she could taste the metallic edge of the saucepan. She could hear coaxing words from Billy. Then the water spilled in her mouth; some of it trickled into her throat. She coughed and spluttered. The violence of her coughing forced her upright and she blacked out again.

Later she would remember moments of absolute clarity. At different times she was aware of Billy and Henry deep in conference, one talking, the other nodding. It was good to know that the world was at last making plans for them. She didn't care what they involved. She had no opinion anymore. Nor did she care what happened to her. There was a terrible stiffness in her neck and shoulders. She was hot, then she was cold. She couldn't move. So she left it to Billy or Henry to throw clothing over her or to mop her brow with a rag that smelt of sea water.

At some point in her fever there were arms reaching under her. She felt herself scooped up and lowered on to a carrying frame of branches and flax. Someone was trying to tip water into her mouth again. She felt it run down her neck. Then she was raised above the sand. She found herself gazing up at the underneath bits of Billy's beard and the cups of his sweat-stained shirt. They left the cave and came out to twilight, and as they walked along the beach, with each footfall she could see the moon gently rise and fall on the edge of the sea.

She heard later of the struggle to haul the frame with her on it up the bluff to the nikaus. Apparently she fell off once but because Billy was smiling when he told her she was inclined not to believe him. Years later she would recall the slow fade of the light in the treetops and the warm tarry aroma of the road when they set her down to rest.

She heard of the questions that weighed on Henry as they drew closer to town. 'What will we say?' And Billy telling him, 'We don't have to say anything. We find the doctor. That's the only thing we have to do.' At one point on the dark road Billy stumbled and fell but somehow caught the road with his elbows and managed to keep the carrying frame stable. She learned later how word got around and people came out of their houses to watch this strange little procession, and of the calm dignity that came over her porters.

− 13 −

'Of course, she married Billy Pohl.'

'Why do you say "of course"?'

'Well, my grandfather had gone. So she married the next best thing.'

'Not Henry?'

'Not Henry. I told you. It was Billy Pohl.'

Rosa's glance was so she could check that the words had arrived safely, that I had heard correctly and what she said required no further explanation. She often did this, her eyes burning into the side of my face until, unable to endure it any longer, I would have to turn my head to look back at her, at which point she lazily lifted her eyes to the road.

'So, this time you hear me,' she said.

This was in the car along the same stretch of coast that Schmidt had made his escape. He had walked with just the moon and the hardness of the road in the dark to guide him. Now and then the sea roused itself. This is what he had told his granddaughter years later in El Imperio across the way from the *cementerio* in La Chacarita. He'd walked in a state of elation. At last he'd escaped the right angles of the sea and the sky and the pinched horizon. At last he'd come back out into the world. Even to the small girl listening his relief sounded consolatory; he'd won one thing but lost another. That other, whatever it was, seemed to lurk behind her grandfather's sad smile. A watery-eyed determination to see only the bright side. The story usually ended the same way. A drum roll of his fingers, a sharp look her way to remind her in case she thought otherwise that he was alert to her thoughts. 'That was the first step I took towards Buenos Aires, towards meeting your nanna and having your beautiful mama. From that day,' he told her, 'my life went forward.'

An icy wind swept up the road, scattering rain across the pavement. There was no traffic, just the dark shapes of the city boxing the wind and the rain. As Rosa turned around from locking up she was surprised to see me still there. She'd offered to drop me off at the hostel before and I had always refused for no specific reason other than a vague sense of pride. That or an inability to accept a favour or kindness. The answer is somewhere in that pot stewing with gruff country-styled living and a certain lack of grace that has to do with youth rather than place.

A gust of wind tore at her coat. She shoved a hand out and turned her face away. Rosa had a way of making the weather seem like some unspeakable insult. I was forever apologising for it.

'Come on, Lionel. Tonight I will drive you. The weather is barbaric.'

The confidence Rosa displayed in the restaurant I saw vanish outside La Chacra. She perched behind the wheel, pushed her face forward and peered shortsightedly. Her foot on the accelerator was surprisingly timid. She was suspicious of everything.

'Where did you say, Lionel? Up this road? My God, it is so steep. They should grow goats here. It is not a place fit for cars. What, here?' She pulled a face at the dark entrance of a track through the bush that was the common shortcut from the road. I knew she would never walk along it by herself.

Two weeks later she would need me on our trip south. She would need me to set against her uncertainty. 'Will it be safe on the ferry in this weather?' (It was raining.) 'Do you think this café is okay?' (Lace curtains hung in the window.) The world threatened in so many ways. The swell in the Strait. The bacterial menace of places we stopped for a coffee and a sandwich.

She pulled on the handbrake and switched off the engine. Discreetly I slid my hand away from the door handle.

'So, Angelo tells me you are going home this Labour Weekend. It is not so convenient to hear this secondhand.'

'It's study leave as well,' I said. I had told Angelo thinking that he would tell Rosa. This is how I thought the chain of command worked. A split second later I realised he had.

'Of course, it is absolutely fine,' she said. 'In fact, I thought we could drive together. I could show you the cave, and also drop you off at your farm. It is on the same road, I think.'

She must have looked up a map and plotted this.

At my hesitation she said, 'That is up to you, of course.'

'Can I think about it?'

'Yes. Of course you may think about it. But you need to know that I have booked the car on to the ferry anyway. Otherwise it is up to you.'

The Rosa that showed up at the terminal looked a different person from the one I was used to. 'Vamp' is not a word I knew in those days. She'd applied a cherry lipstick with a heavy hand. She'd darkened her eyes. She brooded inside a black leather jacket. Under that she wore a fire-engine-red cashmere top.

I saw her before she saw me, and so I stayed put for the moment enjoying this distance and its advantage. She looked smaller, nervier.

When she saw me she stood up, she was so relieved. 'Lionel, I got here early just in case.' In case of what? I didn't ask. There was a moment when she went to kiss my cheek I pulled away. It was involuntary on my part; but only by a split-second. I was sure everyone's eyes must be on us. A 38-year-old woman and a wispy-chinned youth. None of this anxiety and calculation escaped her.

'Look. My Pasta has turned red.'

'No, I haven't.'

'I have embarrassed you!'

'No. No,' I said. 'Not at all.'

And just to prove it I presented my cheek for her to kiss. Only for her to leave my face absurdly hanging there.

'Once is enough,' she said. 'More than that is vulgar.'

She was tired from a late night at the restaurant. For most of the crossing she dozed, knees and arms folded in a big leather chair. I went out on deck. It was October, springtime, and the snowcaps along the Kaikouras were sunlit. Other parts of the landscape still wintered in shadow. In the still glassy waters of the Sounds the tourists came out to the sunny decks and fed chips and battered fish to the seagulls. I leant against the railing and smiled indulgently. It felt good to be out in the world again, away from the sweat and sogginess of the kitchen and the closed atmosphere of the room I shared at the hostel with Brice Johns.

When we rolled off the ferry at the other end Rosa insisted on driving. She hunched over the wheel; gripped it too tightly, and drove too slowly for the straight roads that were magnificently empty.

'Rosa, would you like me to drive?'

'Why? Why do you ask?'

'No reason. I just thought you might like a break.'

'No. I absolutely like to drive.'

She switched her attention back to the road and I slithered down in my seat a bit more. Silence never lasted with Rosa and soon we were talking — about my parent's farm, where it was exactly, what it looked like. I told her and she looked up at the stark bare hills. 'It would kill me,' she said. Her attention drifted back to the road and we entered a new period of silence. Once she glanced at the car clock. She calculated that they would be setting up the tables about now. That cheered her up.

'Kay. What do you think of her?' she asked.

What did I think of her? Kay was emotionally thin. While the rest of us might daydream, Kay gave the impression of total devotion to the task at hand. She was the one Rosa turned to in an emergency. It was Kay who whipped off an old tablecloth, pressed on a new one with gleaming cutlery. The whole exercise was done with chilling efficiency. I couldn't picture Kay outside of La Chacra. I'd heard a husband mentioned; and that he had gone. But that was the sum of my take on Kay. I just couldn't imagine her with a life of her own.

'Kay is totally reliable,' I said.

'She is on the ball, yes?'

'Totally.'

I liked these conversations. They put me above the rank and file and suggested a trust in me that I knew Rosa didn't extend to the rest of the staff. Funny to think that dancing lessons had brought the kitchen and the front of the restaurant together.

'And what about my dishwasher?' she asked.

'Ditto,' I said.

'What is this ditto?'

'It means the same.'

'Ah,' she said, and then something in Spanish that clearly amused her.

'What was that? What was that you just said?'

'Nothing.'

A bend approached and Rosa turned her concentration back to the road. We were about to enter the gorge.

I'd never travelled in my own country with a foreigner before. I found myself feeling anxious. I desperately wanted Rosa to like what she saw. I assumed she would be filled with admiration and that I would feel understatedly proud. Instead, I began to see it through Rosa's eyes. It was big, and shadowed, and above else, it was empty.

Once when we stopped for petrol a tour bus on its way south to the glaciers slowed down. You could see the sleepy faces in the window, dulled by landscape. Already they were sick to death of mountains, lakes, rivers and sea. If only someone would run naked across the street! Their eyes picked me up and put me down again. I wasn't what they had hoped for.

At the end of the gorge we came out to ocean and sky. Rooftops sparkled in the late-afternoon sunlight. As we entered Louise's old neighbourhood of Little River, Rosa pointed to the glovebox for her sunglasses. Private driveways tunnelled through thick, bushy hedgerow. At the top of one drive a rust-coloured metal sculpture showed four spindly figures clinging to one another in a storm of cold green light. We passed a few scratchy streets, a war memorial, and a number of grey weathered houses with murky windows. Little River was one of many towns along the Coast that had earned its living from coal and railways. But no longer. The coal seams were exhausted, and the railway that had carried the coal over the Main Divide to the cities was no longer viable. Weeds grew where the road crossed the tracks. Buildings with Greco-Roman columns and pre-war solidity, once tenanted with banks and solicitors, now advertised bingo evenings. Two women in tracksuit pants guarding a cake stall watched us crawl by.

Out the other side of town the bridge took us across an estuary all golden in the fading light. Up ahead were the jagged black tops of the cemetery. We passed it for farmland. As we slowed down again a cow raised its monstrous head to stare at us. 'Beast,' Rosa said back at it. We drove on.

This is how the Little River Cemetery declares itself, with a small wooden arrow pointing to dense roadside scrub. Rosa had to brake suddenly. She parked the car and we walked along a short path, parting pig fern and bracken until we reached a section of long grass with raised graves, two with iron bedheads at each end. Rosa fossicked around, parting grass until she found what she was after, which is what she meant to show me, in case I thought she had made everything up. 'Here,' she said, crouching down by a river boulder. 'Read, please.' I read out the names of James and Kathleen Cunningham.

It wasn't so interesting, not as interesting as I had hoped it would be. A boulder with a plaque in long grass. But that might have been because I was feeling hungry.

We got back into the car and drove into town. This time there were no false turns. No hesitation at intersections. She drove like a local.

We stopped at a pub to eat, and as I feared would happen, when we entered conversation stopped and faces looked up. Rosa took no notice. It was a younger crowd, some my own age and a little older. Girls in blue track pants. One with a ring through her nose. Another with a nose stud. Some with Chinese symbols tattooed over their arms, or the names of boyfriends branded with 'forever' over their flesh. They were the living, breathing flesh of the land, these large, bloated meat-eating figures with heavy breasts swinging under their t-shirts and sweat tops. Their overfed cheeks sagged on heavy jawbones. In this company Rosa looked like a small porcelain doll.

I bought two beers back to our table. As I sat down she hissed, 'Look at the way these people dress. I shudder to think if I did not provide my waitresses with uniforms. Otherwise, probably they would turn up in rags to wait on tables.'

109

It was the same taut voice we heard at La Chacra whenever a large party of diners squeezed through the doors. When she left her booth it was like the Captain taking over at the bridge. For her to show her face in the kitchen was a sure sign of trouble out front. Friendships were savagely disregarded. A kind word said a moment earlier was forgotten. In the space of a few minutes we had gone from plain sailing to heavy seas, and everyone was required to pitch in. If I was shining wine glasses then I had to be seen to shine more vigorously. Waitresses, as a matter of unspoken accord, were required to show more breathlessness and distress. Angelo's voice rose until he was shouting at the char-grilled meat, hissing at it to cook more quickly. Eventually tables were joined, three clean tablecloths found, the cutlery set and the twenty-six unexpected diners seated, and the earlier calm restored. The waitresses stole out to the loading bay for a cigarette. Angelo stopped shouting at the meat to stare moodily at the grill, and I was left to shine glasses in my own good time. Best of all, Rosa withdrew to her booth of cigarette smoke, and we crossed into the sunset hours of the evening shift.

Here at the pub she pointedly left her cottage pie. She pushed it showily to one side.

I pointed out to her, 'It's a pub, not a restaurant.'

'They still have a responsibility to the food. I would not feed this to pigs.'

She looked critically around at the other tables.

'Look at these people . . .'

I couldn't wait to get out of there, away from the frosty stares of the bar help and the locals.

We got back into the car and went off to find the hotel.

At the desk Rosa turned to announce a slight hitch. 'Well it is not necessarily a problem. They have put us in a double room.' She announced this in such a public way that I could only agree, 'No problem.'

The hotel was a big old wooden one with outside fire escapes, wooden banisters, and a steep flight of carpeted stairs that made you feel you were climbing back in time to mustiness and communal bathrooms. On the landing outside our room she apologised. She said, 'If you are uncomfortable we can change our accommodations.'

'No, this will be fine.'

She smiled. 'Thank you, Pasta. I just don't want you to be uncomfortable.'

'I'm comfortable.'

'I hope it is not too disgusting,' she said, turning the key in the door.

She was pleasantly surprised. There were French prints on one wall. A pouch of pot pourri on the dresser. A stylish bedside lamp. Two beds, I was relieved to see. A double bed and a single which I quickly claimed with my backpack. Rosa looked about for her bag and realised she had left it downstairs. 'Pasta, would you mind?'

At bedtime, she demonstrated the same flair for direction. 'Now Pasta, why don't you use the bathroom to brush your teeth and shower, and I'll follow after.' I did as she instructed. On my return Rosa was in black satin pyjamas. It was her turn for the shower. This revolving door saw me in bed by the time she returned, and the awkwardness I was anticipating neatly averted.

In the morning, we once again had the road to ourselves and once more it was slow going. We seemed to occupy the same stretch of road and the same view without any sense of progress.

I said to Rosa, 'Would you like me to drive?'

'There is nothing wrong with my driving.'

'I wasn't suggesting that there is . . .'

'Then why do you ask?'

Silence.

'Now you're pouting.'

'I'm not.'

'Yes. Your arms are folded. I know that look,' she said.

I laughed, which was a mistake.

'I am also your employer,' she said quietly. And just like that the hierarchy of La Chacra imposed itself on two people in a car driving along the loneliest coast in the world. Rosa was a proud little nation conscious of its borders and entitlements. Soon though she tired of the silence. She sighed a number of times. Then I felt the car slow down. She was pulling over.

'Okay. You drive. I cannot stand your pouting.'

'I'm not pouting,' I said.

'Okay, you are not pouting!'

She waited for me to walk round the front of the car and open her door before she would get out.

'Thank you, Lionel. I remind myself to be patient.'

As soon as she was in the passenger seat she fished around in her bag for her cigarettes. She snatched at the lighter. And when the flame failed she swore in Spanish. She threw the lighter back in her bag. The

112

world was not cooperating today. The view out the window was too still for her, too lacking in stimulation. When a telephone box came in to view she seized on it, sitting up and forward. 'Here. Stop!' She said she needed to call up the restaurant.

She left the car door open so I was able to listen in to her conversation with Angelo. Much of it was in Spanish except for words such as 'mains', 'bottles' and 'cases', and the names of various waitresses. Though once when Angelo had some good news to pass on she shrilled back with pleased surprise, 'Fifty-one shrimp cocktails!' The rest was in Spanish. I liked the transporting effect her language had on me. As with the tango lessons, it was as though I had crept into a corner of the country that no one else knew about.

Now I heard her make noises of condolence to Angelo. I heard her say, 'This country . . .' accompanied by much head-shaking and sighing. And finally, 'Ciao, Angelo.' She hung up and got back in the car, slamming the door. 'One of your rugby teams came in last night. Two of them vomited up Angelo's Steak Argentine. Fortunately it was on the pavement outside the restaurant. But of course Angelo is very upset.'

Your rugby team, she had said. Like when she said *your* country. *Your* people.

She wound down her window and tossed out her cigarette into *my* countryside.

I said, 'You shouldn't do that.'

'What? What have I done now?'

'You threw your cigarette out the window.'

'Oh, I see. I throw a cigarette out the window and two of your mens vomit outside my restaurant. I did not hear you complain of that.

113

I did not hear any apology. And what about Angelo? Have you any regard for his feelings? How he is feeling at the moment. You know how he prides himself. Have you any thought for what he endures?'

My eyes closed on the road.

'Yes,' she said quietly. 'I know how this country works. One little cigarette for two mens' vomit.'

These days a Department of Conservation sign directs foot traffic through the nikaus to a flax-covered headland. From there a track zigzags down to the beach. Once there you can hear the subterranean shift of beach and rock. Every sound bounces off the towering limestone cliffs. Even when it is perfectly still you can sense the experience of huge seas and solitary days lodged in the sober face of all that rock.

The heavy shingle slowed us. Rosa, especially. It was as though she were climbing stairs. She kept stopping to empty her sneakers. She waved her hands at the sandflies. She didn't complain, though. She never said, 'Your sandflies.'

There were other people out and about. Thanks to cars and the DoC tracks this area of coast isn't as remote as it was in Louise's day. Older retired men trudged by with expensive camera gear. A young Japanese couple walked with their arms locked around each other. We approached a boy and girl no older than myself coming the other way. Our eyes sought one another out. As we passed we looked away. I found myself thinking about the girl's face, how fresh it was, and wishing that Rosa had gone more lightly with the lipstick.

We climbed the point into the next bay and dropped down to the

114

rock pools where Louise had bathed. We walked on. At a midway point I went ahead. Already I could see the cave entrance. I wonder if it isn't more obvious now than it was in Louise's day. The stench of urine hung around the entrance. Next to rockband graffiti the names 'Tosh' and 'Liz' were scrawled inside a large crudely drawn heart.

I waited for Rosa to catch up, then we pushed on through the dark, using the curve of the cave for guidance then there was a greyish light and an eyelid view of the ocean. We craned our heads up at the pitched roof. We were in the right cave. This was it; we were there in the story.

To the rear of the cave Rosa began to casually clear sand with the toe of her shoe. Then as she seemed to realise what it was she'd found she got down on all fours to sweep away the sand. I helped her. Once we had exposed the old dance floor we stepped back to admire it. We stepped on to the rock, then, quite naturally, as we might have at a late hour at La Chacra, we began to dance. There were no bold moves. It was more of a shuffle — the kind of thing I imagine Billy Pohl might have favoured. So we shuffled. Slowly. And it was easy because it wasn't really us at all. For that moment at least we were Louise and Schmidt.

Something like a step or a turn brought our faces closer, and without any fuss or hesitation we kissed on the mouth. Rosa's lips tasted of cherry, and they were full — the lipstick did not lie. It truly represented the area of her lips. We parted. Rosa smiled. Then she kissed her fingertip and touched my lip, her face broadening to a new warmth. She took my hand and appeared to be dallying with a thought; then she closed her eyes and pressed my hand against her chest and dragged it slowly down her front. The dumb hand of the shellfish gatherer and the wilfulness of the other.

I might mention here that with Rosa there was never any mistaking her pride when she spoke of her grandfather. When she stood before his photo on the restaurant wall you could see her positioning herself in his history. She was his granddaughter so it was no surprise that the grainy texture of that past should project through her. Once she moved away from the photos, off location as it were, she became herself again, restaurateur, employer, dance instructor, illuminated by lava lamps and nasty brickwork.

In the cave I was witness to another shift as she tried to fit herself in to Louise's life. Was it in order to see her grandfather more clearly? And was the kiss just a bridge? I wasn't sure.

My relationship with Rosa already had so many forms and now we'd just created another. As a result of that kiss I was sure I would find the world a changed place. But how to re-enter this world? How would we leave the cave?

In tango it is the man who initiates and the woman who reacts. I should have known that with Rosa established protocol didn't always prevail, that she would take care to see us out of this moment.

When she had taken my hand she had turned slightly away, her face closed with concentration. There was a rapid breath like the one I had heard from her on the stairs back at the hotel. It was as if she was reaching for something, and then having made contact with it, she gave a contented grunt. Now that she had arrived at that place she had privately wondered about all these years she switched her attention to me. She looked surprised to see me there. 'Hallo!' she might have said, as though this was an unexpected encounter in the street, or in a supermarket aisle.

She reached up and gave my cheek a playful squeeze. She grunted. So, we had been playing after all. It was safe to leave the cave now. We were back to restaurateur and dishwasher.

On our way back to the car our sides touched and I remembered the Japanese couple. We walked with the same sort of attachment, slowly and contentedly in the shingle, and in the same direction as Billy Pohl, Henry Graham and Louise when they left the cave.

That night she falls backwards on to her bed, the toes of her shoes pointing up at the ceiling. She looks like a small black and white doll. She raises a hand to her forehead. A tired gesture, the kind that a performer might make when at last they find themselves offstage and all alone. She closes her eyes, and when she draws her fingers back through her hair I can see the white flesh and the thick dark hair of her underarm. Now her eyes snap open and I see the whites and blacks of a magpie. She seems to know what I have seen and what I am thinking and feeling. She chuckles and smiles. 'Pasta,' she says. Her eyes which so often contain a hundred practical restaurant matters begin to focus on me. She is drifting, I think, between appraisal and a decision, and at the same time covering up that process by pretending to find me amusing. The thing is, I want to kiss her. I want to return to that moment in the cave and by the fastest route possible. She must see that, and as I teeter at that employer-employee threshold, Rosa reaches out to me.

'Why don't you come here,' she says.

Why don't I? And because I feel the need to say something, anything at all, I say, 'We could dance.'

That amuses her.

'Thank you, Pasta, but no.'

She sits up then and begins to scratch at her back for the zipper on her dress. I move across to help her. Kneeling on her bed I run the zipper down her back and as her dress parts a sweet perfume escapes her.

Afterwards, we lay in our separate dark. For some reason I found myself thinking of Brice Johns and his pimply face stuck in one of his economic textbooks. Of course I had moved on. That's what Brice was doing in my thoughts. I had moved on into new territory that Brice could only gape at from afar and wonder. I wished he could see me now. In bed with Rosa. I was exhilarated. Sleep was as far away as ever. At an early hour I heard a train haul through the middle of the hotel. With the peace restored I moved on to my other side, then back again, until I heard Rosa say, 'For godsakes, Lionel, go to sleep.'

– 14 –

I RANG THE FARM AND GOT MY MOTHER JEAN. SHE SOUNDED ANNOYED
with me. She had been expecting me the previous night. She had even
rung the bus company to see what time the bus would come by and
then driven out to the road to wait for the bus to drop me off at the
farm gate. Towards the end of this recitation it occurred to her to ask
what I was doing on the Coast?

'I'll explain later,' I said.

'Well, what bus will you catch?'

'I won't be on a bus. I'm driving.'

'A car?' She sounded puzzled. 'Whose car?'

I was calling from a phone box and I was aware of Rosa studying
me through her sunglasses. She was sitting in the passenger seat. That

was another of the changes that last night's event had racked up. At breakfast she had deferred to me. 'I think I'll have an orange juice. No, an apple.' She couldn't decide. She said, 'Lionel, you choose for me while I go upstairs.'

I said to Jean, 'Just somebody's. You'll meet them soon.'

Them, I said.

'When?' she asked.

'This afternoon.'

'When this afternoon?'

'I don't know. Some time.'

I hated it when she tried to pin me down like that. Her need of scheduling. This excitement over my homecoming. It just made me deliberately more vague. I hung up and left the phone box and got back in the car.

'So, everything is okay?'

'Yes. Everything is okay.'

'Do we have time?'

'Yes,' I said.

We drove round to Louise's boarding house. By now it had turned into a backpacker's. We sat outside, glancing up at the windows. We debated whether to go in. I couldn't see much point. Its only unusual feature was that it had two storeys. By Little River's standards I suppose it had a certain structural grandeur. Otherwise its colour regime kept faith with the same flat white that you saw up and down the street.

I trailed Rosa into the reception area. She asked if we could look in the rooms. She didn't say why and she wasn't asked to explain herself.

It all seemed perfectly reasonable to everyone concerned except me. A young woman in jeans, the manager, showed none of my embarrassment. She handed Rosa two sets and pointed the way up the stairs.

The house was a shell, stripped back to its fundamentals. Its hallways were used to the bruising and bumping of packs. The carpet was worn down the middle. Rosa opened the door to the end room and made her way to the window. She stood there gathering views. A sense of the boundaries that had locked in Louise's life is what she was after. The dark ranges in the east; the woolly morning cloud that caught on them. She fished in the near view, the house across the road, its sodden clothesline, the windows that were still in shadow.

That's pretty much how the rest of the morning proceeded, with me keeping up some kind of sentinel presence on this mission of Rosa's to feel her way in to Louise's old landscape.

To catch up with Louise's ultimate rejection of it we had to drive up the coast another fifteen kilometres, to the line of old miner's cottages on the beach where Louise had lived with Billy Pohl for a while. All these years later, solo mums from the city had moved in and painted gardens on the weatherboards. You could see the withering effect of the harsh sun and where the petals and flowers had lifted off in the summer humidity. We stopped and parked outside a cottage; its corrugated iron had been painted purple. When we got out of the car Rosa went directly to the letterbox, which blossomed with a large sunflower.

'How old do you think this letterbox is?' she asked.

Like the house it was a metal box and it perched on the gatepost.

'As old as the house,' I thought.

This was the kind of confirmation she was after. The letterbox went into her carpet bag of fact and memory.

In the front windows we could see our reflections. It didn't look like anyone lived there. Rosa wanted to go in and look around. Once more she deferred to me.

'We have time? Yes?'

'Yes,' I said.

We let ourselves in the gate. I closed it after Rosa. We walked along the side of the cottage to the timeless sound of the sea washing up a shingle beach. Around the back a line of flax separated the ocean from the back door. Rosa sat on the back step and lit a cigarette. She patted a place by her, shifted a little to make room for me. I sat down, our shoulders pressed together. She put her arm around my back and squeezed me towards her. A faint perfume leaked from her woollen jersey.

'You are happy, yes?'

I smiled and nodded.

We sat in silence for a bit.

Then Rosa said, 'I wonder if this place is for sale?'

'Would you buy it?'

'Maybe. Maybe.' Then just as quickly she decided differently. 'No. I do not think so. I don't like other people's castoffs. Secondhand clothes. Things. This place is like that.'

'How so?'

She stabbed her cigarette out on the porch and immediately lit another.

'Let me ask you a question.'

'Go ahead.'

'Have you ever had a pen pal?'

'Yes.'

I surprised her with that answer. But my mother used to encourage me and my sister Megan in this area. Jean had a pen pal in Canada she wrote to for years until one day the woman's husband wrote to say that she had been killed in a car accident. Megan wrote to a girl in Spain and an Australian boy living in Port Moresby.

'And you?'

'Jules. He lived in Ottawa.' He had sent me a photo of himself ice skating and I sent one back of myself on a horse.

'And this Jules,' she said. 'Supposing for the moment it was a Julia who once you had loved. And she asked you to come and live, where did you say, Ottawa, would you drop everything to do that?'

She saw my confusion. 'Never mind,' she said. She felt around for her cigarettes. They were in the bag, and she'd left it in the car.

'Lionel, would you be a sweet?'

It is 1919. Louise stands by her letterbox looking at her first letter with foreign postmarks. She weighs it in her hand. It is light as a feather. A short letter. The piano tuner acknowledged the point himself. It was just to re-establish contact. He promised a fuller account once he heard back from her.

Immediately she wanted to write to him. She wanted that contact. But then she thought, what's the point? It would just reopen an old wound. He had hurt her. He must have known that. Besides, an ocean separated them. She screwed up the letter. Within the hour she was searching back through the rubbish to retrieve it. This time she set it alight so Billy wouldn't find it.

Sweeping up the ashes she regretted the finality of her action. She hadn't written down Schmidt's address. She'd left herself without any possibility of a change of heart. And of course, no sooner was Schmidt's letter a pile of ash than she felt that change of heart. She regretted it the day after, and for weeks after that. Schmidt had given her a rope with a hook to haul in the horizon and she had rejected it.

Another six months had passed when a young man in a suit showed up to her door.

'Louise? Louise Cunningham?' he asked.

She went by the name Pohl these days but she nodded.

The young man introduced himself. He was the new piano tuner for the Coast. She could have saved him the trip. She didn't own a piano anymore. She was about to tell him as much when he mentioned Schmidt.

'Mr Schmidt. Paul Schmidt has written to ask that I give you this.' It was a letter. As she took it from him he said, 'Mr Schmidt wasn't sure you were still at this address and so wrote to the firm asking us to verify.'

Even on the page he was able to gently chide her and make fun of her anger. He managed to do so without raising his voice. He was quick to tell her how much he missed her. He missed their dancing. He missed her eyes, her hair. He missed the feel of her. She had come to fill in that place that he had carried around inside of himself during their time together in the cave. She had usurped a country-sized craving. In Buenos Aires he lived with the constant thought of her. At any time of the day or night she was his companion. And on a more playful note he was happy to report that she was alive and well in Buenos Aires. In fact, he said, she was 'thriving'. He may have been joking but she felt her face light up when she read that. Schmidt was also anxious to know how her days in the cave had ended. If she would write and tell all he would reply immediately.

She waited a day, then she decided to wait another. In the evening she watched Billy by the fire turn his clothes on the drying rack. He looked so gaunt. It was that hour when his chin turned blue, and the day's labour left him looking drained. The steam off his clothes brought back the hideous nature of the mine, its cruel procedures and Billy's role.

That afternoon she had walked up Paradise Valley Road to watch the pit ponies dip their heads in the fields; it was their last day after a month in the open air. She had watched Billy fit on their eye pads and lead them back down the hole in the earth. A month earlier she had stood with schoolchildren behind a rope as the poor animals were brought to the surface. A small girl had touched the nearest pony and left a small handprint in the coaldust.

In the morning she sat on the back step to write her first letter to Buenos Aires.

She told Schmidt about falling sick in the cave and how she'd woken up in hospital to the fresh smell of linen, the sound of trolley wheels creaking in the corridor. For several days tubes carrying a saline solution ran in and out of her veins. She was badly dehydrated. She wondered if he remembered the policeman who had come to her house. Well, he had also visited her in hospital. It was the same old Ryan, awkward, officious, uncertain. He leant over her bed with his notebook. He wanted to know if he could ask her some questions. She said he could if Tom Williams was present. He gave her a strange look. She heard him say, 'Tom Williams is dead.' Then as he realised he was breaking news to her, he said, 'Dear Christ, I'm sorry, Louise. Tom suffered a heart attack back in early December.'

She chose not to tell Schmidt she was married. But she mentioned Billy Pohl and Henry Graham in passing. How they had sat out the rest of the war in a camp at the foot of a windblown mountain. She told him of the kind acts she was treated to when she got out of hospital. Neighbours had brought her food. In the Little River Cemetery Jackson had come over with his paper bag of sweets. 'I saved you a caramel.' Audrey gave her a hug. She told her, 'Jackson kept your grass nice and trim.'

Louise's first letter ended with a request. She asked Schmidt if he would trace out on paper the dance steps he had taught her. She wanted to practise them. She had one other thing to ask. In the future, he should write to her care of the local post office.

Schmidt's letters filled in another world for her. And of course they supplied her with new dance steps. A Portuguese furniture polisher who lived beneath Schmidt complained of the floorboards creaking above his head. The furniture polisher had the feeling that the world was sneaking up on him. But Schmidt couldn't put the steps down on paper until he'd traced them out on the floor.

How odd it was to contemplate that bad relations between tenants were all a result of a woman's requests from the other side of the world. To Louise it was reassuring. Schmidt's descriptions of his irritable neighbour had her believe that despite all the distance separating them, their lives could still impact on each other.

Schmidt sent photographs of himself. He asked for the same from her. With a pair of scissors she cut Billy out of one of the studio photos and sent that.

For the next few years they exchanged letters. Her relationship with Schmidt continued as it had always done — as something half-realised, a glimpse that strives for more.

In the sitting room Louise rolled back the rug and set about following the latest steps Schmidt had written down. She attached the notes to a broom. It saved her going back to the letter whenever she lost her way. This was adequate for a while, but then she found herself wishing that the broom wasn't merely a broom, that it offered more presence. More possibility.

One morning down at the beach she happened to spy a ketch; its sails were down and as soon as she saw the cross hatch of the mast and rigging she knew what to do. She hurried back to the cottage and hammered a piece of wood across the top of the broom and hung on it one of Billy's jackets.

Schmidt possibly never knew the value of his letters or the extent to which they sustained Louise and nurtured in her a capacity for a parallel life. In one letter she asks him to write less frequently. She is afraid of arousing suspicion at the post office. As it is she always watches the postmaster's face whenever she asks, 'Anything for me?' The slightest smile may mean more.

'Let's see. Yes. Something from your pen pal, Louise.' Each time is cause for fresh surprise. Year after year, surprise after surprise. Mail is bounty. It is treasure to be parcelled out. Every new letter she takes to the beach, to a log she snuggles up to. She reads quickly to the end to make sure there are no unwelcome surprises, then she goes back and reads slowly, digesting each morsel. A silken feeling bloomed inside her when she read how much Schmidt missed her.

She stowed the letters, along with the photos of Schmidt, in a cake tin which she hid under the front steps.

She gave Billy no reason to suspect that the piano tuner was still part of her life. She even felt secure enough to buy a map of the world at the church fair, and bold enough to pin it to the wall above the kitchen sink. It was three days before Billy even noticed it.

'What's this, then?' he asked.

'Just to show where we are in the world,' she said.

She watched Billy's eye skate across the pale blue Pacific for South America, then stop and pause before drifting south to the pink and white cap of Antarctica.

At night they lay in bed in wakeful silence. She waited for Billy to raise himself on to his side, and with a big 'oh well' sigh reach for her. He wanted a baby. She kept putting him off without saying why, exactly.

'There's nothing wrong, is there?'

'No, Billy, it's not that.'

She couldn't say what it was either. It was just a feeling that once she had a baby with Billy her correspondence with Schmidt would have to end. That thread would be severed. She would have responsibilities, loyalties of flesh and blood to consider.

She had come a long way in her private world. The experience of the cave had made her aware of the layers people wove about themselves. She could lie next to Billy and dream of another man. She could cross the floor with a cup of tea for Billy where just an hour earlier she had danced with Schmidt's stand-in. She could stand idly dreaming before the map of the world and when Billy came up behind her and placed his hands affectionately on her waist he would have no idea where her thoughts were or who her smile was for.

It was an unsatisfactory life, of course. A wallpaper life interweaved with too many bright smiles. She began to feel a disgust.

One afternoon she deliberately left the dance notes taped to the broom and when Billy turned to ask, 'What's this?' she said, 'What does it look like, Billy?'

His face appeared stricken for thinking what he did. He started to say something but swallowed that reply.

'They're just dance steps, Billy. I've got no one to dance with.'

As soon as she said the word 'dance' she saw his thoughts rush back to the cave. She saw the same urges rise in him. The wanting. His doubting. For a second she thought they might actually dance. But then the hand holding the broom fell at his side. Billy was simply unable to lead.

Instead he mentioned the name of a woman, the wife of a workmate. Dottie Fearnley.

'Dot says the curtains are closed here during the day.'

'That's because I dance with the broomstick,' she said. 'You wouldn't want someone looking in and reporting back to you that your wife's gone mad.'

'Well, has she?'

She saw him grin.

'Well, maybe just sometimes, Billy.'

'Sometimes is reasonable,' he said.

In 1924, Schmidt wrote asking her to come to Buenos Aires. He wanted her in his life. But he couldn't wait much longer. She must decide. The letter also contained the news that he'd started a business, 'importing bandoneons'.

Louise stood at the back door with Schmidt's letter. This was the fifth time she had read it. She arrived at the word 'bandoneons' and looked up and stared through the clumps of flax at the shredded ocean.

The end came unexpectedly.

Most of the mail passing through the post office was domestic. A great deal of it related to the mine and the government department that managed it. Leading up to Christmas, volume tended to swell with packages from the United Kingdom and Australia. In the new year it quietened down to the regular correspondence. Letters from Argentina were always likely to catch the postmaster's attention.

He was a small man with an eyepatch — he'd lost his eye in an explosives mishap up at the mine. He also hobbled, though no one knew why. His hobbling and his eyepatch contributed to Louise's idea that he might be discreet, so when he mentioned his stamp collection she was happy to steam off the stamps and give them to the postmaster.

In 1927, to celebrate the non-stop flight of Charles Lindbergh across the Atlantic, Little River held a 'kite day'. The celebrations included wood chopping, a cake fair, some local knitting and crafts and the postmaster's stamp collection.

At the miner's hall Billy found himself in the crowd moving past the tiny colourful postage stamps set against a white mount — a fresco of British Royalty figures, fantails and kowhai, and more un-expectedly, the howler monkey, the giant ant-eater, the condor, the rhea, Iguazú Falls and José de Martin, the military hero of Argentina. All this was merely interesting until Billy caught sight of Louise's name in the postmaster's acknowledgment thanking all those 'whose correspondence made the display possible'.

Billy walked home. He let himself in and sat down in his chair. Louise was in the kitchen, her back to him. Over her shoulder he could see the map. This time his eye stopped at the tail of South America. The rest of the landscape and ocean, he now realised, was diversionary landscape.

Louise was chopping up beans when she heard Billy call to her, a quaver in his voice, like he got when he was trying to sound firm with damaged goods taken back to the shop.

'Louise, I want to see the letters.'

Whenever she had imagined this moment she had always thought she would pretend not to know what he was on about. But when she turned from the chopping board and saw his dark face she felt the full brunt of his knowledge. That was the first thing. The next thing she saw the hurt in his face. She had never wanted to hurt him.

'I'm sorry, Billy. I'm so sorry.'

He looked away, his eyes blinking.

'I want to see them,' he said.

She said, 'They're under the house.'

Later she wondered why she hadn't lied. Then she thought she was glad she hadn't.

She said, 'They're private letters, Billy.'

'I know that. I didn't say I wanted to read them.'

She left him in his chair, his legs apart, hands on his thighs, staring into space. She was only gone a minute. The cake tin with the letters was under the front step. When she came back inside she found Billy was buttoning up his coat.

'This them?'

He took the lid off and looked in at the pile of seventy to eighty letters. It was enough to see them. It near took his breath away. Now that he'd seen the letters, the sheer number of them, he put the lid back on and handed her the tin. He gave a curt train conductor's nod and moved towards the door. It was getting on for dark. She called after him, 'Where are you going, Billy?'

'I don't know, yet,' he said.

He didn't come home that night or the next. Then, in the early hours of the third day, she heard a movement inside the house. She sat up in bed and saw Billy's coated figure dart across the bedroom door. She heard him moving things about, the sharp sound of a chair leg drawn back. Once he coughed.

She got out of bed and pulled on her robe. In the main room she felt the cold air from the open door. She went to close it, but was diverted by a half-empty cup of tea. She went to pick it up and that's when she saw the pile of money. She didn't like to touch it. She'd never seen so much money. Billy saved her the task of counting it. He seemed to emerge from a corner of the room. 'There's four hundred pound there. It's yours.' He told her he would go away for a few more days. 'That should give you enough time.'

Billy's gesture wasn't immediately obvious to her. The pile of money. This talk of his disappearing for a few days.

'What about all this . . . money, Billy? It didn't just fall out of the sky.'

'No it sure as hell didn't,' he said.

He seemed preoccupied. He glanced around the room as if checking to see if he had forgotten something.

'I was happy here,' he said. 'I don't know how it will be with you gone.' He closed his eyes. It didn't bear thinking about. He took a deep cleansing breath. He said, 'I want you to be happy, Louise. I want it more than anything. I had thought . . . well, I was hoping, wasn't I? I'd hoped you'd forgotten him. I don't know, Louise. I don't know what's right here, to be honest. Maybe it's unfair to ask anyone to give that up.' He shook his head down at the floor. She went to touch his arm and he glanced away. His gaze stopped in the door of their bedroom. Their life together briefly flashed in the air.

'Jesus,' he said.

She tried reaching for him again. She wanted to hug him but he stepped away. He made it clear that he wanted it to happen this way, and his way was to believe in the practical nuances of instruction, and the painlessness of following things to the absolute letter. That was Billy for you.

When she saw him move towards his packed bag she got to it first. She wanted to do things for him, help him through, which was as well because Billy had closed his eyes. She had to pick up his bag for him. She had to close his fingers around the handle. She told him she would never forget him.

He nodded, with the slightest glimmer of a smile.

'I know that,' he said. He turned to the door. 'I'm going now, Louise. I don't want to open my eyes. Just turn me around so I face the gate, if you don't mind.'

She'd seen Billy do this same thing with the pit ponies. Blindfolded, they had followed trustingly after Billy on soft knees for the black hole in the ground. She took hold of his sleeve and turned him for the door, guided him down the steps. He stumbled once and she caught him.

'I'm okay, Louise. I'm okay.'

He meant her to take her hand away.

'Goodbye, Billy,' she said.

She watched him walk slowly to the gate and let himself out. He closed it behind him. She saw he still had his eyes closed. She watched him walk along the fence with his face turned to the cottages on the other side of the road.

It was the last time she would see Billy Pohl.

THERE AT THE FARM GATE WAS SOMEONE WHO LOOKED LIKE MY FATHER, only older and more dishevelled. He didn't recognise the car or the occupants at first.

Peter's elbows fell out of an old green jersey. It was his favourite. To this day, in fact, whenever I think of him he is dressed in that same threadbare jersey. The missing elbows weren't something I would normally have noticed in the past. But I was seeing my father through Rosa's eyes. And frankly, I was also a bit annoyed to see him there. The farmhouse is at the end of a long drive in from the road and I'd hoped for a moment alone with Rosa before she drove on to catch her boat. But there was my father, as he had always been, only more embarrassingly so, moving amongst the mud-splattered cattle towards the driver's side of the car. A look of boyish delight on his red face.

'Lionel!'

He dropped his face down in to the driver's side window; it was much too large and rural. Then he saw Rosa, and it was as though a rare animal had flitted across his vision. He quickly recovered and reached past me with his large paw. 'Hallo. I'm Lionel's father. Peter.'

This was the first time a friend or acquaintance of mine had been invited to call him Peter. In recollection I think he'd noted everything in a single glance, and just like that, I too found myself upgraded in his eyes. That evening was the first time I would call my father by his first name.

As Rosa got out of the car she paused to take in where we lived. The razorback gullies, the slips and burnt hilltops where my family had farmed for more than thirty years. And as she started for the driver's side Peter said, 'Come down to the house for a drink.'

Rosa glanced at her watch. She looked to me for a lead. I didn't want her to come in to this area of my life where all the trappings of my childhood would be available to her. What if she had a change of heart? I didn't want to risk any re-evaluation on Rosa's part. But I said, 'Sure, if you've the time. You can meet Jean.'

This was also the first time I had called my mother by her first name. My father smiled. He tapped the roof of the car. 'You get back in and drive down to the house. Jean is there. She'll fix you up. I'll be along as soon as I'm finished with this lot.'

As we nosed our way through the heifers I looked up and in the rear mirror I caught sight of my father leaning on a manuka staff and gazing after us. He was trying to arrive at some kind of conclusion. I had seen him search the skies in the same kind of way, sniffing out 'the weather', trying to second-guess it. The man I saw in the rear mirror I thought looked confused and slightly awed.

We drove down to the house and parked by the shed. Over at the kitchen there was a movement in the window. My mother would have heard the car. She would have seen the unfamiliar vehicle winding down the hill. The front door opened and she hurried down from the porch, her face filled with questions and happy surprise. When she saw Rosa she quickly adjusted.

'This is Rosa, Mum. This is Jean. Rosa runs the restaurant I work at,' I told her.

'No,' said Rosa. 'The truth is your son runs it. He, alone. I am the lucky one.'

I saw my mother catch the foreign accent. She wiped her hands on her dress.

'Oh,' she said. 'Well it's nice to meet you.'

Rosa ignored Jean's offer of a handshake and kissed my mother on her cheek. My mother blushed and smiled. Quite unconsciously she raised a hand to her cheek where Rosa had kissed her. And it struck home, perhaps for the first time, how isolated my parents' lives were. In the past, whenever people raised this with my mother she would point to the mobile library, the telephone and the television. She kept in touch, she liked to say. But it was always from a distance. Around people she and Peter became uncertain. They turned adolescent, bashful, apologetic.

Jean herded us in to the kitchen and there I discovered the 'new thing' in my mother's life.

Stuck to the cupboards, the fridge, the door and the light were the words — *sego, si ranko, porda, lumo.*

'I've decided to learn Esperanto,' said my mother.

'Esperanto!' What a joke, I thought. What an embarrassment. And, more importantly, what would Rosa make of this?

'It's a language,' said my mother firmly. She looked to Rosa for support.

'Yes. Yes. Of course. I recognise these words.'

My mother smiled at Rosa and cast a look of quiet triumph my way, as if to say, 'Well, there you are.'

Rosa's behaviour was even more unexpected. I had never seen her so anxious to please. My mother smiled sweetly. Rosa smiled sweetly back. She wanted my mother to like her.

I went out to get my bag from the car. On my way back I met Rosa in the hall. She was looking at the photos lining the walls. Dull images, worn by time. Photos of how the farm used to look; photographs of Peter and Jean in their younger days, of me and my older sister, Megan when we were little. Rosa peered more closely.

'This is your sister, Lionel? This one?' She pointed to Meg when she was fifteen. She is on her favourite horse. In the same photo I'm sitting on my pony, Meads. My father tended to be the one who named the animals on the farm.

'That's her.' I didn't point out me.

'She's very pretty.'

She looked at her watch and said she had better get on her way. She didn't want to miss the boat. The way Rosa drove there was every chance of that.

My mother was aghast. 'What, now? No. No,' she said, and Rosa laughed.

'That's what your husband said.'

'Peter?'

I explained that we'd met him out at the gate.

'Well, Peter is right. You can't go. You just got here.' She looked for something to take off Rosa, her handbag, her woollen buttoned-down top.

At that moment my father pushed the door open. He stood on the step. The outdoors seemed to cling to him. He smelt of the hills, his hair pushed this way and that by the wind. My mother said to him, 'They just got here and now Rosa is leaving.'

'No,' said my father, stepping out of his boots. 'Stay the night. You can pick up the boat in the morning.'

That was true, as it happens. It made no difference to Rosa whether she got back to town that night or before noon the next day.

Rosa checked with me.

'Sure. We've got room, Rosa.'

'Room!' boomed my father. 'We've got rooms to burn. There's Meg's, the spare, or the study . . .'

'Meg's, I was thinking,' said my mother quietly. She could have been considering where to place new furniture. To Rosa, she said, 'We would love you to stay.'

'Thank you. You're both very kind.'

The compliment made my mother's face red. She turned to my father and he sprang to life.

'Right. A drink. I'll take care of it.'

139

I noticed he winced as he moved past us in the hall. I watched him hobble to the door at the end.

My mother spoke quietly, so Peter wouldn't hear. 'It's his hip. The doctor said he needs a replacement.'

I saw her look at me to gauge the effect of what she said. I felt a panic rise in me. And I'm ashamed to say it wasn't for my father's sake, either.

'Well, we find out next week,' said my mother.

Before dinner there was a knock on my door. I didn't answer it. I was sure it was Rosa, and I didn't want her to see my bedroom with its swimming certificates, old school photos and posters of pop bands that no longer existed. That was the old me.

The new me was unveiled after dinner when Rosa, in full flight on trails from Buenos Aires to La Chacra, to family history on the Coast, suddenly blurted, 'You know, your son is a very good dancer.' Peter peered at me over his tea cup. I saw in his eyes the stranger I'd become.

'Lionel is?' asked my mother doubtfully.

Now Rosa said, 'Lionel, there are some tango tapes in the glovebox.'

'Tango,' said my father. He sat back in his chair and grinned at my mother. 'I'm looking forward to this.'

I went out to the car and got the tapes. We pushed back some of the furniture. My mother stood up from the table to watch. My father poured himself another glass of whisky (he filled Rosa's glass too) and stayed at the table.

The tape started with the slow, sensuous 'Mi Buenos Aires Querido'. It is difficult to convey the strange dislocating effect of that sound in the isolated farmhouse. Years later when I was to show my sister Megan where we danced that night she stared at the floor then out the window at the bare hills unfolding to the horizon and shook her head. She couldn't grasp it.

I placed my hand on the small of Rosa's back and we began to dance — slowly. Rosa closed her eyes, and for the benefit of Peter and Jean I tried to look disengaged; as though it held no more joy for me than washing and drying the dishes. I'm not sure I succeeded any more than Schmidt and Louise did in the cave the time when they had danced in front of Billy Pohl and Henry Graham. Once I looked over Rosa's shoulder and saw my father's mouth ajar and from my mother a look of awe that I felt had to do with things other than dancing.

'Mi Buenos Aires Querido' ended and my mother applauded. There was a 'bravo' from Peter. My mother came forward. She laid her hand on Rosa's arm. 'That was the most beautiful thing that I've ever seen.' She turned to me. 'Lionel, you didn't say. You didn't even write about this.'

'He's been taking lessons,' said Rosa.

'Lessons!' boomed my father from the table.

'Yeah. I'm sure I mentioned it,' I said, even though I knew I hadn't.

The tape moved on to 'Buenos Aires Conoce'. This time Rosa encouraged my mother on to the 'dance floor'. She motioned to my father. 'You too, Peter.' And when he was slow to move from the table she slapped her thigh, and to my surprise he rose like a big woolly farm dog obedient to its master's voice.

'We are all going to dance,' announced Rosa.

My father made a scoffing noise. My mother shot him a look of impatience. 'Just listen, please, Peter.'

We began with some stretching exercises. Rosa wanted Peter and Jean to understand posture. She drew her hands above her head, like someone embarking on a swallow dive. She said to my mother, 'I want you to imagine you are reaching up to a lower shelf in the kitchen.' My mother smiled compliantly. My father half-heartedly leant his hands against the cupboard door. 'Now I want you to imagine you are reaching for the spaghetti at the back of the shelf.' My mother stood slenderly on her toes. My father stuck out his stomach in the belief that this extended his back. We had our spaghetti now and we eased back to normal standing positions.

'This time,' said Rosa, 'I want you to think of yourselves as water pipes. She turned to me for clarification. 'Water pipe? This is the word, Pasta?'

My father blinked at me through the bars of his arms. This was the first time he'd heard my restaurant nickname.

'Water pipe. Down pipe. It's all the same thing,' I answered solemnly.

'Thank you.'

Rosa turned to my parents. 'I want you to think of water going up and down the pipe. I want you to listen to it. It will keep you straight because what happens if you bend forward?' My father went to answer but Rosa answered for him. 'Yes. You get a kink in it and the water does not flow. So. I want you both to think of yourselves as water pipes.' She motioned my parents towards her. 'Peter, come here, please. Jean.'

My father limped over. My mother smiled up at him. Rosa arranged them. She got them to stand more square on. She placed my father's big unfeeling hand on my mother's back. I had never seen my parents actually learning. Like all children I assumed that they knew everything they needed to know in this world. Now I saw the keen way my mother lapped at new information; and the slight self-doubt that nagged in my father's face.

Rosa clapped her hands as she did in the restaurant whenever she wanted everyone's attention. 'Okay. I think this. Lionel, you take Peter over there. And I'll go through *basico ocho* with Jean, please.'

'*Ocho*,' said my mother adventurously. 'That's Spanish for eight, I believe.'

'*Bueno, bueno*,' answered Rosa.

My mother smiled back at my father. '*Bueno*. That's Spanish for good.'

I slipped in to the role of Mr Hecht and got Peter to stand behind me and copy my steps until we laid the *ocho* down. As he counted the steps I offered encouragement. It felt as unnatural as any other reversal. The father is the one who usually casts the shadow. The father is where knowledge begins. My father concentrated like he did when looking over the possible purchase of new farm machinery. His eyelid lowered in the mechanical act of committing everything to memory. Whereas across the room, my mother held her mouth slightly open to catch every word of Rosa's instruction. 'Okay,' I said. 'Let's try it again. One back, across, lead with your left . . .' Peter grimaced whenever he moved his right leg. He had to drag it into place, then extend his left toe as I had done; because of his big woollen jumper that skirted his hips

143

there was something absurdly female about his efforts.

From across the room Rosa clapped her hands. 'The ladies are ready.'

'Oh Christ,' muttered Peter.

'You're fine,' I said.

'More like a sick old sow,' he answered.

Rosa switched the tape on to 'Los Argentinos' and we danced.

'They are enjoying themselves, yes?' she said of my parents. She was justifiably proud of what she had started here.

Halfway through the tango Peter and Jean began to argue.

'You're throwing me off balance, Peter.'

'That's because you're trying to move before I'm ready.'

Rosa said something sharp in Spanish for my ear only. She gently shoved me aside to sort out my parents.

'The man moves. The woman responds. It is a conversation. The man may have his opinion but he must respect the other, yes? It is the same thing.'

'See,' said my mother.

My father rolled his eyes and started over to his whisky glass. Rosa grabbed his elbow and led him back; she placed his hand on my mother's shoulder.

'You don't move until I do,' said my father.

'Peter, please,' said my mother.

This time my parents followed me and Rosa around the room. They trailed after us for two more tangos, I heard my father's heavy breath, my mother's gentle corrections, the slow drag of my father's gammy leg that threatened to pitch the farm and my own future in uncertainty.

Megan's room is next to mine. In the middle of the night I heard the light go on and Rosa get out of bed. Her shadow crossed the doorway. Her footsteps trailed up the hall for the bathroom. On her way back she looked up to find me waiting in my doorway. She clasped a hand to her chest. 'Lionel, you gave me a fright.' She reached up and kissed me warmly on the mouth. Then a peck on my cheek. 'Good night,' she said, and because she knew what I had hoped for, she added, 'This is your parents' house. We must respect that.'

In the morning I was still in bed when I heard her out in the hall on the phone talking *rapido* to Angelo. I hurried into my clothes. I was too late. Peter and Jean were already standing at the door. It meant I would have to share Rosa's departure with them.

'*Adiós,*' said my mother.

'*Muchas gracias,*' replied Rosa. 'You are learning.'

She kissed both my father's cheeks. Peter blushed.

My mother suddenly remembered the tango tape.

'No. It is yours. A gift,' said Rosa.

In amongst all these formalities she squeezed my hand, a melting smile, then she drove to the main road, back out into the world.

I sat at the same desk I had studied at for my school exams. Only now the desk top rubbed against my knees. I threw myself into legal systems. And when I came up for air I found an empty world. Yet it was the same world no less that had entertained me in the growing-up years. I bounded up hills which in my childhood I'd named after mountains. On top of these wind-blown slopes I gazed at more of the same, hill after hill chipping away against the grey sky. As a child the view had

145

suggested everything that was enormous and unknowable. Now the same landscape seemed diminished and foolish. It didn't know anything except fertiliser and weather.

Of course I was missing Rosa. I missed her terribly. It was only a week, but coming after the events of the weekend it was a long time to be apart. Whenever I took a break from study I stood in Meg's room inhaling the Tosca brand of perfume Rosa sprayed between her large, comfortable breasts. I went back over the events of the weekend. The kiss in the cave might have been part of a Rosa-conceived experiment to slip inside Louise's shoes. Even the big event in the hotel room may have started out the same way, but I didn't think or feel that that was how it had ended. The new Rosa, the demure Rosa, was proof of that.

I brooded, and generally stonewalled Peter and Jean's efforts to humour me. I let them know I was studying. My head was crammed with the 'do or die' facts and cases of legal systems. My mother came in with sandwiches for the 'worker'.

'*Surprizo sinjoro,*' she said.

I don't know why, but her learning Esperanto infuriated me. It was such a dumb thing to do. I baited her mercilessly. She resisted, in her quiet way. She said it was an established and legitimate language.

'Okay. Tell me this. Where in the world can you order a cup of coffee in Esperanto?'

She thought for a moment, swallowed, and said she was not going to defend something that was 'self-evident' to her.

At dinner she and Peter asked after Rosa. Was she married? 'Was,' I told them. Or was that 'still is'? Come to think of it, I wasn't sure of

Rosa's exact marital status.

I said, 'I really don't know that much about her.'

My mother glanced across the table to my father. It was his turn to take up the inquiry.

'She's an interesting woman, all right. And you work at the restaurant?'

'I'm the kitchenhand. I told you. You know that already.'

I got up to leave the table.

'We're just interested to know about your life, Lionel,' said my mother. 'We're not prying.'

'We're just being parents,' said Peter.

Late one morning I came back from a walk to find Chrissie Wheeler in the kitchen talking to my mother. Jean looked industrious and pleased with herself. Scones were baking in the oven.

'Lionel, look who's here,' she said.

She gave Chrissie a slight shove that she wasn't prepared for and poor Chrissie took an odd, stumbling step towards me. Immediately she wanted to swim back to the bank from which she had been pushed. She blushed back at Jean. Her face lit up in an eczema red. She pulled a strand of light brown hair across her face and smiled shyly at me.

'Hi Lionel. I heard you were back.' She looked at my mother when she said this.

Smiling to herself Jean went on stirring the soup with a wooden ladle.

She said, 'The scones won't be ready for another twenty minutes. Why don't you two go for a walk?'

Chrissie must have sensed my reluctance. For that matter I made no attempt to hide it. She said, 'Maybe Lionel has study or something to do?'

'Nonsense,' said Jean. 'Off you go.'

I was glad to get away from the kitchen and the clumsy matchmaking efforts of my mother. We took one of the farm tracks. I'd known Chrissie all my life. Her parents had a farm farther up the same valley and were firm friends of Peter and Jean. The Wheelers used to come over for cards and games evenings. On occasion Chrissie would sleep over in Meg's room. We had played games over the same tracks we now walked along as two adults — or at least one of us was, Chrissie, as I thought of her, was still on the cusp. Away from Jean's custodial eye she was full of questions. How was I finding the city? University? Study? Not too hard, was it? Was it easy to make friends? She kept brushing her hair back from her face and when she did that I caught a whiff of fresh shampoo. She even smelt young. She couldn't leave her hair alone; that nervous gesture and her slender legs tucked into tight jeans, made her feel so much younger and more junior than myself. Our sides touched. And when Peter came motoring along the track, home for lunch, his big rumpled face smiled at what he saw and at what he and Jean plainly hoped for.

Over lunch my parents did all the talking. Chrissie hid behind her hair.

'Chrissie, did Lionel tell you he's learning tango?'

Chrissie stole a quick look at me, 'Really?' her youthfulness bolting ahead. She quickly retracted and crept back behind her hair and said, 'I mean, really?'

I nodded down at the scone I was buttering. The table lapsed back into silence.

Now I heard Jean say, 'Lionel, why don't you show Chrissie some steps.'

'We don't have any music.'

'We do. We have the tape that our visitor left behind.' Our visitor. She wasn't going to mention Rosa by name in front of Chrissie.

'Chrissie doesn't know the steps. You have to know the steps.'

'Exactly,' persisted my mother. 'That's why I thought . . .'

She was interrupted by Chrissie.

'No. No. Please Mrs Howden, it's all right.'

My mother ignored her.

'Lionel?'

'She doesn't want to,' I said.

My mother put down her bread-and-butter knife and gave me a cold look; Peter placed his hand on her hand and gave it a tender rub.

So I said to Chrissie, 'Another time.'

The week dragged on. In the afternoons when I took a study break I went out on the farm with Peter. His leg was a dead weight to haul behind him or hoist on to the farm bike. It was a shock to see how reliant he'd become on the bike. All the time he complained of his 'bloody leg' and how it restricted him. He couldn't drop down a hillside anymore. It wasn't just the loss of mobility; it seemed to me that my father had grown older. His loyalty to the same old overalls and green jersey meant that they too accompanied him on this aging journey. Those big holes in the elbows of his jersey. A safety pin held together

149

one of the shoulder straps of his overalls.

These bare hills I had grown up in had turned my father into a cripple and my mother into a social isolate. And for what? It made no sense to farm, none whatsoever. It was a crappy business as far as I was concerned. My father just smiled. It didn't seem worthwhile to him to point out that he did what he did because that is what he'd done all his working life. Financially though it had become harder, a lot harder. Everything about my parents lives was fraying. There were no more government subsidies to fatten the profit line, no more residual youth and energy to call on. My parents were just one of many smallholders whom the government had deliberately closed their eyes to and probably hoped would leave this marginal land behind and let it revert back to whatever it had been three generations before.

Peter's justification was peasant simple. 'You can't remove what is in your blood.'

Old instincts and established routines and hoary old attachment to the land were justification to continue. Jean had her own reasons. In her case, the world was just the right distance from the farm gate. She preferred to read about it and listen to it on the National Radio. 'I guess we're old dinosaurs.' She smiled when she said this, happy to be a dinosaur.

Now with the benefit of hindsight I see more clearly what their attachment was all about. It was to each other, mediated through the farm and its routines. My father wasn't like the neighbouring farmers who stayed out all day. At one o'clock Peter arrived in the door for the soup Jean had simmering on the stove all morning. I remember once when school finished early on the last day of term Megan and I stormed in the door to what we thought was an empty house. We went into all the rooms calling for them until finally there was a sheepish reply from their bedroom. Our father came to the hall in his woollen farm socks and heavy trousers, tugging on his belt, red-faced and a little amused. He offered some lame explanation about their feeling 'tired'. Meg and I crept to our rooms for 'silent reading'. We knew we had disturbed an area of our parent's lives which we were expected not to think about. The only solution was to mark out our distance again and wait in our bedrooms for the dinner gong to bring us back together.

On my last morning I stood at the window watching Peter drag his leg on to the farm bike. My mother crept up behind me. For the past few days I had sensed her wanting a moment alone.

'You know Lionel, your father won't ask for your help. You know that, don't you?'

She joined me at the window.

She said, 'If he has that hip operation there's a recovery period. The doctor says he's not allowed to do anything.'

She went on to say that he was on the hospital waiting list. The hospital chose the date for the operation, not them, and unfortunately, as it happened, the date pencilled in for the op fell smack in the middle of docking and shearing.

She said, 'I hate to put this to you . . .'

I couldn't bear to look at her. I couldn't let her see just what a huge thing she was asking me to give up or to see how desperate and impatient I was to return to the nights at La Chacra. I couldn't wait to get away from their slow, shambling lives, and the door view of my mother propped up in bed, with her Esperanto book held open at a tilt and the sibilant nonsense rising from her mumbling lips as she plodded along lines of language that no one really needed to know or wanted to understand.

– 16 –

DEPARTURE IS SUCH A DEFINING ACT. HENRY GRAHAM'S FAMILY GAVE AWAY their beehives to a widow. The house they disassembled to a pile of weatherboards; just an old concrete washing tub was left standing. Billy Pohl took from the cottage only what he could carry in his coat pockets. He left in the dark so the neighbours wouldn't see him. He walked all that day and through the night. He wore out three pairs of shoes until at last he'd walked all the way south, as far as Riverton, where he sat on the rocks and searched the horizon for Antarctica, then slipped his shoes back on and started north. He kept walking until he had walked out all his grief.

Louise also travelled lightly. She arrived at the railway station a full two hours before the train was due to depart. She just couldn't wait to get on her way. She didn't want to linger a moment longer in her old life. The station master ventured out to exchange views on the weather. It was her last conversation in Little River. 'They say a southerly is on its way . . .' Years later, whenever she thought of Little River, first stop in her memory was the station master's red face, his pale blue eyes, and the rocking motion with which he held himself.

In Buenos Aires, Rosa's parents, Roberto and Maria, spent nearly a month selecting pieces of furnishings, sorting, itemising, and arranging for their despatch.

This was Rosa's father's idea. It seems that he had woken one morning with the need to do something dramatic in his life. Roberto wasn't his father's son for nothing. Yet he might be criticised for having left his run a bit late. He was nearly sixty. Until now, it had been a sedentary life. Everything had been carefully laid out ahead of his arrival. Into this space his father created Roberto had slipped effortlessly, as if of right. But it was a hand-me-down life, the music business not his but his father's. His father's ambition, his empire. And finally its demise had been Roberto's to oversee. Six shops devolving to the one. The raft that sustained them shrinking to a few bare timbers. Aside from these business misfortunes other tensions waged in the air. The sabre-rattling of the military. The wanton violence of the Montoneros, their scoffing rejection of everything bourgeois, old money, family cartels, American business. The demonstrations grew rowdier, the confrontations more violent. Bombings were frequent.

One evening Roberto invited Maria and Rosa to hear his plans. They repaired to the living room. A large inflatable globe stood on a glass-topped coffee table. Roberto blew evenly on to the Atlantic

Ocean; the globe began to spin, and eventually came to rest with his finger on Sydney. It was the only flamboyant act of his life, apart from his death.

In the course of packing up for their new life in Australia, Roberto came upon a cache of letters in an old safe. For years a potted cactus had sat on top of the safe gathering dust. No one had seen the old man open the safe. No one even thought of the cast-iron box as a safe place for valuables. It was just the place where the cactus sat.

Here were the letters Louise had written to Schmidt. As well, Roberto discovered a number of letters to Louise from Billy Pohl that had fallen into Schmidt's hands following Louise's death. Louise's own letters to Billy Pohl were to end up with the director of the cemetery out at Chacarita.

One letter stands out above the rest. They say it's always the letter that fails to arrive that carries the weightier news. This letter, written by Rosa's grandfather, had been stamped 'return to sender' by the Little River post office. Louise had already left, and so several weeks later Schmidt had the painful experience of reading back to himself the news he'd intended for Louise.

He'd been unable to wait any longer.

– 17 –

Rosa once said that every change of dance partners brings something new out of you. A new way of being, a new way of moving. An entirely new compass is put in place. The same might be said of countries. 'Think of the country as the woman and the immigrant as the dancer weaving new steps and patterns upon her.' Rosa was quoting a famous poet.

At Montevideo, after three long weeks at sea, Louise left behind the spacious decks and games of Patience for the crammed immigrant boat and its reeking cargo on the final leg up the Rio de la Plata.

It was late October. The air was warm. 'Congenial', she'd later write. And after weeks at sea, with just the horizon to concentrate on, land was jammed with detail. She left the Neapolitans, the Galicians and a number of German families with their luggage piled on the wharf, and on unsteady legs set off across a wide dusty road to a row of motorised cabs. She went to the head of the line and showed the driver a slip of paper with Schmidt's address.

Soon the taxi left behind the bustle of the port for the quieter residential streets and the bridal formation of trees. The taxi passed in and out of their shade. Louise gazed up at the icing cake friezes on the building façades. It was roughly as she'd hoped. The layer upon layer of new sensation. The new life arriving effortlessly, like a well-managed stage shift. She couldn't stop smiling. Eventually the taxi drew up outside a pink two-story house. There was no garden. The house was flush with the street and you entered through a door off the pavement. She noted its cheerful colour, the jagged cracks in its plaster exterior. With a start her eye stopped at the black shuttered windows. She'd reached a stage in the journey that she hadn't properly thought out. So much energy had been invested in her getting here that now she had arrived, the shutters had a cautioning effect on her. They were a domestic detail that raised questions about the piano tuner's new life, things to do with privacy and matters undisclosed, the unsaid things that live in the margins of letters.

The driver tilted his head back and waited. He spoke in Spanish. Then he turned himself around and spoke in halting English.

'Señora, this is the address.'

Once more Louise looked up at the shutters, then back the way they'd come. She seemed to remember their passing a hotel.

'Si. Viejo.'

Viejo Hotel on Defensa. This is where Louise's Buenos Aires story begins.

For a number of days she laid low. The several weeks at sea had left her feeling weak. Her stomach was in disagreement with something she had eaten or drunk. She sat in the shade of her room while she thought about how best to insert herself into the piano tuner's life. At home she would have sat by a window looking out at the wind and rain and it wouldn't have occurred to her that there was another way; that the partially glimpsed is oddly more satisfying. She liked the shutters. At least she liked the idea of them. She liked their hard ruled lines of light. It was as though the day itself was measured. Take this amount of light only, as in a prescription. She smiled. She had just thought of a way to begin a letter to Billy Pohl.

At night she sat beneath the hanging plants out in the courtyard with the other hotel guests, drinking tea, listening and smiling perhaps a little too hard through the conversation of others.

On her third day in Buenos Aires she decided to leave a note for the piano tuner. That way the next step would be up to him.

On the evening of the fourth day a hotel worker handed her a business card — *Paul Schmidt. Importer & wholesaler. Specialist in musical instruments.*

'Señor Schmidt is waiting at the gate.'

She stood carefully, the way she had observed of the other women, as though rising to one's feet also meant gathering up all one's worldly possessions. She was also aware of the interest from the hotel staff. Their olive faces glowed in the gas light, alive with the prospect of something consequential about to happen.

The last time she saw Schmidt he was bearded, in ragged trousers and bare feet. So it took a moment to adjust to the view at the far end of the courtyard. The snappy whiteness of a summer suit shifting behind the gates. As she approached she noted the changes. The piano tuner was plumper than she remembered — though in a prosperous way. The skin beneath his eyes was moist. She had an idea that he had just hurried away from a big dinner.

'Louise?'

His voice, too. His voice had changed. It was more accented.

She nodded and smiled back at his astonished face. That too was not as tanned as she remembered.

His hand reached through the bars of the gate to touch her cheek.

'My God, Louise,' he said. 'It is you.'

Schmidt told her she looked exactly the same. She hadn't changed a bit.

'Not a bit. Not just a little?'

'Not a whit.'

This was in bed in the grandeur of the Hotel Madrid where they lay amid wreaths of white sheets, their flushed faces staring up at the ceiling.

Their initial excitement is easily imagined. The assignations. The meetings. The embraces coming after so many years apart. The shared sense of waking from a prolonged coma and a determination to reclaim what had once worked for them in a cave half a world away. They took walks and meals together. Schmidt made her laugh. He spoilt her. Opened doors for her. He made space in his life for her, generous space.

But ultimately it was to be a compromise of sorts, with Louise learning to share Schmidt with a woman he never spoke of. It would be a life spent in the margins of another's life. Furtive. Secretive. Life in fact as they had known it in the cave.

– 18 –

SCHMIDT HELPED HER TO FIND LODGINGS. AFTER THE VIEJO IT WAS A STEP down to rooms off narrow corridors, and noisy courtyards. A whole community gathered behind a single door facing Avenida Almirante Brown in the neighbourhood of the port. Here, smiling Italian women gossiped about the European stranger. The woman without language. The woman without a husband. The woman without children. A woman three times struck down by lightning.

It was the little things that she was learning to claim. She loved the kitchen window. The old sprigs of rosemary on the tiled sill. The window frame with its flaking paint. The security of the sill, the way its bevelled edge helped to locate her, steadied her for this next moment, when she pulled back the window and opens the shutters to the blinding light. The sheer volume of things foreign suddenly pouring through — the block of sky, the foreign curses flung across the courtyard, and below, the mêlée of terrified chickens and the shouts of children out in the street, and the strange birds that sat in the boughs looking back at her.

She felt like a child, learning things over again. Their names. The different weight of things said and things meant.

Schmidt's efforts to teach her Spanish were unsuccessful. She shook her head and made up excuses. She was too old to learn. She was English. Besides, the one person she wanted clear understanding with understood her perfectly.

So, at the *pasteleria* she might point at trays of pastries that looked like deep seashells with custard filling; likewise at the *parrilla*, at the item she had bought on other occasions. She pointed and pointed and if she was feeling bold that day, where she pointed she sometimes stuck a word. As soon as she opened her mouth to speak the others in the shop turned their heads. Who was this strange fish that had swum into their waters? Sometimes she would flush out an English voice. More often it was someone wanting to show off or practise their English. 'Please, the señora wishes for a piece of the lion.' The world was all the more interesting when not fully comprehended. She smiled graciously. *Gracias. Muchas gracias.*

This was life in the margins of language. In the margins of Buenos Aires. In the margins of Schmidt's life. Nonetheless it came as a shock when Schmidt told her of his wife's pregnancy.

Along with her regular pastry shop and *parrilla*, there was the Astride in Montserrat. She turned up there and waited for Max to bring her an absinth. Max was a short tubby man, his face oval and thick-skinned with discretion. Things said stayed secret with Max. He also had an extraordinary capacity to answer back any kindness shown him, his face bursting alive. She enjoyed watching him strut about the bar, the boyish pride with which he wore his money belt. It hung off his bulging stomach like a gunslinger's holster. The way he expertly anticipated his customer's requests, the chess enthusiasts too engrossed by their game to look up and signal more coffee. As the shops and offices emptied the bar filled. The drinkers kissed his cheeks, and behind his glasses Max's green eyes would develop a reef of light, a pearliness settling along the tops of his stained teeth. She heard someone call him Max and so the next time he brought her over her drink she was able to say, 'Gracias, Max,' and witness the heavenly glow that recognition brought to his face.

She sat up to the window trying to concentrate on the night settling in the trees and rooftops, watching its slow spread to the street. She was trying not to think of Schmidt at home, kneeling by his pregnant wife, rubbing her swollen ankles and feet. She finished her third absinth and Max brought her a copper tray of peanuts. Since by now the bar was quiet he pulled up a chair and listened to her talk on and on; and why not? Drink stripped off her layers as it did with everyone else. Max was a good listener. He nodded at a surprising number of right places. He responded to the nuances by sighing and shaking his head. He brought her a coffee and a piece of torte. She talked. At some point he got up to pour her a brandy. A little nightcap never did anyone any harm. By now the hour was late. Only the chess players remained as he pulled on his coat to walk her to the bus stop. 'Bub bye, Louise. Bub bye,' his chubby hand waved. *Bub bye.* Words Louise had taught him. At home, she walked straight to her Victor RCA.

– 19 –

EVERY CLOUD HAS ITS SILVER LINING. THE PREGNANCY AND SUCCESSIVE others saw Schmidt's wife give up her day-to-day duties in the business. Schmidt waited until he felt the time was right, then casually announced without fuss or fanfare that he thought he'd found a possible replacement. A quiet, able woman. A foreigner. A weary sigh departed him as he said this. 'I don't know if it will work out. We'll have to wait and see.'

In 1932, Louise joined Schmidt's staff where she remained to the end.

During the day, she worked shoulder to shoulder with Schmidt. At night, they danced *milonga*, pressed together like a clothespeg.

Over the years, at Christmas and at other busy times, Schmidt would employ more assistants. These intrusions were temporary and Louise accepted them with indifference. She had seen such help come and go over the years, and one more eager-to-please face cannot break down the knowledge that this newcomer, like all the others before them, is simply filling in time and space.

Without another life to divert her she poured herself into Schmidt's business.

Among the staff she was known as the reliable one. The trusted one. At the end of the day she scooped out the takings and counted the notes and coins into neat piles of separate denominations. She knew the business backwards. Her knowledge was deferred to. The new assistants were directed to ask 'Mrs Cunningham'. 'Mrs Cunningham' was the filing system. She was the store. This quiet, unassuming presence rarely spoke. She saw to the paperwork. She dusted. She filled in orders in her neatly scripted English. She visited the Customs Authority. There she did business with the clerk, an elderly poet who had once visited Edinburgh, and who looked forward to her coming so he too could practise his English, sometimes reading to her from *Treasure Island*, the poet standing to recite. Louise seated, her ear cocked ready to correct pronunciation. R.L. Stevenson was the custom clerk's favourite 'Scottish author'.

For her part, at the shop Louise was deliberately courteous in an old-time employer-employee way. She was always careful to address the piano tuner as 'Señor Schmidt'. Never 'Paul'. She often had to repeat herself. Then it would be like soft rain falling, so quietly did she speak. 'Señor Schmidt?' Until finally he turned, perhaps a little surprised to find her standing there — his 'pale moon'. It was the end of the working day. City faces hurried past the front window. Heads inclined, some holding the brim of their hats.

'Ah, Louise.'

Here it was — a quiet acknowledgment won. Automatically Schmidt looked for his wife who unexpectedly had dropped in. The Señora was in his office on the phone talking loudly to her friends. The sound of her voice left him momentarily disoriented. It often happened like this when Louise and his wife were in the same room. His wife was the one to suddenly change into a foreigner. Now, turning back to his 'shop assistant', he saw the dust mites hanging in the air. The years piled up between. Her face, as always, was resolute, betraying nothing. Her thin pale lips barely moved as she spoke the name of the subway station and the time.

At a later hour, on the platform beneath Avenida Corrientes, the subway roar was deafening. People bumped in to one another and the mouths of these reef fish moved in voiceless complaint as they shifted around a middle-aged man in a dark coat with his arms wrapped around a thin woman standing half out of her high heels.

Once a year Schmidt would visit Colonia in Uruguay. His wife usually joined him for the trip to the quaint Portuguese settlement across the River Plate. There was a musical instrument business on Avenida General Flores and two more retailers upriver in Montevideo, for whom Schmidt was the agent and supplier. Bandoneons. No one could get enough of them.

The first year his wife was pregnant Schmidt went alone. The following year found her burdened with baby. The city sagged under a heatwave. No one moved if they could help it. Señora Schmidt sat in their shaded apartment. The thought of the three-hour boat journey made her shudder. She couldn't possibly go.

Schmidt complained in a quiet, grumbling way. He alluded to the various functions he'd been invited to and for which he needed her to be there. 'Well,' she said. 'Why not take the moody shop assistant. She could use some fresh air.' Schmidt pulled a face and walked over to the window, his heart in a flutter. Beneath the window, the park. Beyond, the river. He looked without taking in anything. There was a general impression of browns and greens, of a world poised for rearrangement. Now he heard his wife come up behind him and place her hands on his shoulders. 'Just this once,' she said.

It would be the first of many trips to Colonia. Schmidt arranged rooms at a different address to the one which he and his wife had stayed at in the past. At the dead end of Calle de España, a cobbled lane dropping down to the water's edge, on the top floor of a three-story *casa*, Schmidt and Louise raced each other to close the shutters.

They slept through the hot afternoon. At night they picked their way over the cobbled streets with other holidaymakers. They walked slowly, arm in arm, both feeling young again. Louise delighting in the genteel ruin of the old town. Schmidt too, feeling the bloom of youth upon him, once put his back out when reaching up for a branch of flowering japonica. No matter — it was just a muscle spasm. Smiling bravely he squeezed out the perfume between thumb and forefinger before planting the stem in the top buttonhole of Louise's white blouse.

To onlookers they must have seemed like a couple uncommonly absorbed in each other; not your average honeymooning couple for whom the candle burns brightest at that one showy moment, but then not typically middle-aged either. Look at how the señor assists the señora over the roughly paved *calle*. Look how he bends to kiss her cheek. Look at how they dance, his cheek pressed next to hers.

Schmidt kept his appointment on Avenue General Flores. He turned down the rest of his social engagements, complaining that he felt unwell, listing the heat and his nervous digestion, then spent three more days idling with Louise, at the end of which he left to make his rounds in Montevideo, leaving Louise to wander at her leisure around the yellow railing that traces the Colonia waterfront, and to stab her finger at the offerings listed on the menu.

– 20 –

IN BUENOS AIRES, SCHMIDT'S WIFE TOLD FRIENDS OF HER HUSBAND'S 'convulsions', his flip-flopping in bed. 'He worries too much. The business. *The business.*

It is always on his mind.' Insomnia. It was the devil's curse. There was a time when she wondered if he was possessed. She consulted an Indian shaman who instructed her to crush the eggshell of a particular bird in to Schmidt's coffee. She followed the shaman's directions and watched for her husband's reaction. Schmidt raised his cup, tasted the coffee, swallowed. She saw him reach a hand to his throat. He coughed once and worked his mouth to get rid of the grittiness. Angrily he asked if she had put salt in his coffee. But nothing else came of it. Schmidt did not expel the promised egg with its captured troubled spirit. And his restlessness continued.

While the rest of the city slept she lay in bed listening to her husband stalk around the apartment, his slippered feet laying trails of insomnia about the place. She told her friends he wore out the carpet between the kitchen and the window. She heard him switch on the jug. The low murmur of radio music. *That* dance music he always listened to. A cough. A sigh. And finally the snip on the door as the insomniac let himself out into the night. She understood that he had to do something with himself. He had to get out and about. He reported back to her, somewhat shrilly, there were others similarly affected. The pavements were filled with people like himself. Night people. Insomniacs who stopped one another to exchange a word or offered a passing nod of recognition.

The routine was well established. Schmidt would walk several blocks from the apartment on Avenida del Libertador, perhaps stop in at the all-night bookstore run by Felipo, a friend of his wife's. It was, a useful alibi, and not too much of a nuisance. There was always a book of numerology to discuss or a tall tale to hear from a Bolivian's volume of stories. Afterwards he'd walk another block, turn down a side street for a door with a red light, outside of which there was a taxi waiting to drive him to one or another *milonga*, though nearly always in Almagro, a neighbourhood that his wife and her friends never went near, and where, he knew, Louise would be waiting for him, in a chair by the wall, politely declining all offers to dance, her eyes on the door; and at every new arrival looking up hopefully for the flash of silver hair.

In future years . . . whoever thought that a 'three-minute affair' would stretch so far? In future years, on Sunday afternoons, Louise and Schmidt would meet down at the waterfront where a long rickety pier probes like an index finger the muddy waters of the River Plate.

Louise was usually the first one there. There she is, sitting on a bench waiting for Schmidt to extricate himself from his comfortable apartment on Avenida del Libertador.

He always hoped to see her first. Sometimes he did, and these days hobbling on bad knees he stops to squint into the untrustful distance, admiring the view. The way the river air pushes her skirt against her legs. To his eyes Louise is still young, forever young; the sight of her still excites. On the other hand, the same view can produce a moment's regret where he feels intensely her exile and solitariness. Once she told him she'd been a victim of a pickpocket. She went on to describe the feeling of a 'fish nibbling in her coat pocket'. A fish. And just like that his memory tore back through the years to Little River with its lapping tide and crayfish pots.

The other thing he saw at this distance was her containment, the same thing that you see in nuns and old men for whom the world they move through is not nearly as important as the one they have carved out within. With Louise there was always that other place that she would not always share, even when he tried to draw her out: 'Why, my dear, are you so sad today?' Sad? She looked up and saw the piano tuner's loving concern for her. And as easily as that, responsibility shifted. Now it was her turn to act light, to laugh or pass on an incident. Or simply shrug and say, 'No reason,' and to go on staring at the shifting water.

Schmidt would have suggested a café in Almagro or one of the many parks were it not for Louise being so insistent that they meet at the pier. It's easy to see why. At the end of the pier you find yourself searching for the horizon. And tucked behind the horizon was the old life Louise had left for this one. The pier was their place. It is also the place of Troilo's signature departure piece, 'Danzarin'.

This, along with the rest of her grandfather's collection would pass down to Rosa.

- 21 -

In Sydney, a younger Rosa trawls through the letters. She begins to unpack memories of the strange old woman who worked in her grandfather's store. She is old enough to know the whole story now. And, she is like Louise now, isn't she? Young. In a strange country. Without a local's grasp of the language. She is struck by the similarity of their circumstances. Someone else has trodden this same road.

It's here, on the other side of the Pacific, in her new life, that she begins to reconsider the woman she knew as 'Mrs Cunningham'.

Mrs Cunningham was always polite to her, although her smile was a bit quick, not quite securely fastened. She was always in a hurry to turn back to her book-keeping. Nor did Mrs Cunningham have any of the questions which adults usually hold in reserve for children. How is school? What's your favourite subject? She resorted to none of the easy flattery. I bet you are the cleverest in your class. No. Children have a way of sniffing out the genuine interest from that which is faked. But Louise was a rarer species still. She didn't care, and nothing pricks a child's interest more.

Rosa would stand outside the door marked 'Mrs Cunningham', daring herself to knock. She never did. She could never quite bring her fist to strike against the stained wood. Her purpose was too vague and uncertain. She wouldn't know what to say to 'Mrs Cunningham'.

Then her death, followed by her grandfather's depression. She listened in on her parents' talk. When she tried to find out more they said it was nothing. But if it is nothing, then why were they talking about it in that way?

'Poppa is sad.'

'Poppa is sick.'

'Poppa has lost his faithful lieutenant.'

Then her grandfather's death and the revelation that the outward signs had not been reliable. 'Mrs Cunningham' had tucked in all her overflowing bits to make sure that nothing would give her away. In control at every moment; filling in that space the family accorded her with cordiality and good grace. 'Mrs Cunningham' had been a fake.

In Sydney it is hard not to feel a fake. It is difficult to pretend that you belong when clearly you come from somewhere else. When you don't understand the language. Roberto's finger had come to a halt on the globe a bit too easily.

Schmidt Musical Instruments & Importers is resurrected on a busy road in Parramatta. For days on end Rosa's father stands behind the counter watching the buses and the foot traffic. Whole days pass without a soul entering the premises. The phone never rings. Rosa watches her father turn a little greyer, and his eyes grow dim with the sad lesson learnt. The name Schmidt and its long association with musical instruments does not invoke the same respect as it did in Buenos Aires. In Sydney there is not the same tradition to trade on. After six months of dismal takings the shop closes and Roberto and Maria open an 'ethnic restaurant', the Almagro Steak House on Bondi Road.

When Rosa isn't waitressing she is dancing at the academy in Leichardt. Her dancing pleases her parents. Thank God something of the old country has survived. She is still her grandfather's girl after all. Roberto's hope is that she will meet a nice Australian boy. What better place than a dance hall that offers proper supervision? Roberto has met Mrs Redmond, an impressively framed woman whose blonde-tinted hair rests in coils, pile upon pile. She is exhausting just to look at.

Roberto has yet to notice the dishwasher, a boy two years older than Rosa.

The first time Rosa introduced herself she had to get him to repeat his name.

'Ivan,' he mumbled.

'Ivan. Please, did you say Ivan?'

She had to peer up under a fringe of hair. Like lifting the lid off a pot. As soon as she comes into the kitchen his eyes lift out of the sink. The rest of him is immobile. Only his eyes move, shift, follow her. And whenever their eyes meet he never blushes. He is shameless in that regard; a mystery, but a good worker. They are never out of plates or saucepans. And every night he leaves the kitchen area spotless.

At odd times during the day she begins to notice him. In Leichardt as she is climbing the steps to the academy — there he is, moving out of the corner of her eye. When she stops to look properly he is gone. She starts finding him on the same bus. She looks up from the Spanish bookshop and the movement in the window is him, his narrow shoulders, the mop of untidy hair, the Janola-splotches over his jeans.

She sees him when she least expects to.

In Hyde Park, the national flags are flying. Yugoslavia. Italy. Greece. Ireland. Chile. Argentina. The dancers are dressed in their respective national costumes. The Greeks in white tunics. The Irish jiggers with their freckled faces. Every nation is roughly as expected. The Yugoslavs Slavic. The Italians wilfully homogenous. No surprises so far, as the National Australia Day crowd shop around, squinting in the bright sunshine. Though she feels like she is at the zoo, that she is one of the creatures, it is nice to be noticed for a change. That's when she sees him; pushing foward from the edge of the crowd.

At the first resonant bars of 'Danzarin' an excited woman cries out 'Look!' and the crowd switches its attention to Rosa, sitting crosslegged on a wooden traveller's chest. Her face is pure white. She looks like she's never been touched by sunlight. The next thing they notice is her bob of black hair — jet black. Once upon a time a crow must have swept down from the tree-tops and nested. Her eyes are too big, and what people say about thin arms would also appear to be true. They

177

just make a face look sadder. Rosa's white arms dangle out of a dress made of silver fish scales, and when she stands to walk to her partner she shimmers. She is fish and water in one. As she meets her dance partner and places her hand against his she is thinking of the mop of hair peeping over a shoulder in the crowd.

That night at the restaurant she confronts him.

'You were at the park today.'

'No,' he shakes his head and looks vacant.

'I saw you. I was dancing and I saw you.'

'Nope,' he says. 'Must have been someone else.' And this time his face plunges down into dishwashing sink.

It is towards the end of the night. Rosa is reaching up to put the cups and saucers on the shelves when she hears her name called. For a moment she thinks it is her father or perhaps someone from the academy has come to look her up. But it is Ivan.

'Yes,' he says. 'You did see me.'

He doesn't look apologetic. It's the same impassive face that greets good fortune and disaster equally.

Good. She knew it was him. But she doesn't feel triumphant. And Ivan looks far from vanquished. Nevertheless it represents a breakthrough of some unspecified kind.

The next day she bounces up the steps of the academy in Leichardt and there's Ivan, brazenly sitting on the edge of the steps. Right there in her frame; not to the edge. He rises slowly to his feet and gestures vaguely.

'I thought I'd like to learn,' he says.

There is time to notice his teeth. He has good teeth, which is a relief. At the dance academy she often finds herself paired with older, European men whose gums have retracted, their teeth outlandish, almost tusks. Or those with tobacco stains and sour breath. 'One or two of them may try to brush against your tits,' Mrs Redmond has warned her. 'There's always one to try it on.'

In the mirrored dance room it is Ivan's youth that catches her attention. The way he holds his arms high as if strings are connected to his hands and she is his marionette. Or as if there is a river running between them. His face is taut with uncertainty. He keeps apologising, Sorry. Sorry. Sorry.

That night at the restaurant she comes into the kitchen to see him tracing out the steps to *ocho basico*. He hasn't quite got the sixth and seventh step right. She is showing him this when her father, flushed, sweating in his chef's high white collar, sweeps through the door and stops short. His face turns a deeper crimson. Ivan releases her. He feels like the dog that is found playing with his master's shoe. He returns to the sink, head down, his cheeks that chalky white.

The following week she has to tell Ivan that he can't attend the classes at the academy anymore. Her father has spoken with Mrs Redmond and told her in no uncertain terms that it isn't 'a proper relationship. It is not suitable.'

Rosa would like to argue with him, not because she feels anything for Ivan, but because of the principle at stake here. Her mother neatly anticipates this and cuts her off.

'Rosa,' she says, and it is the tone that carries the message. Anything for peace; that, and her mother's face, with its collapsed ridges and dashed hope, which prevents her speaking out.

Besides, these days her father isn't his usual self. He is depressed. He is drinking more. More than is good for him. The path of least resistance is the desired path at this point. She understands. The compliant nod is for her mother's sake.

As a result, Ivan creeps back to the periphery. That's him seated to the rear of the bus she takes. And there he is, again, in the corner of her eye as she mounts the academy steps. It is Ivan's shadow that passes in the window of the dress shop.

Her mother has asked her to accompany Roberto to a soccer match. It will be like the old country. The pitch with its familiar markings and boundaries. The call of the referee's whistle. Perhaps Roberto will forget himself, and his depression disperse in wave after wave of the crowd's cheer?

The two sides are ancient foes in the local competition. One is predominantly Greek, the other Turkish. And within moments of the game starting a Turkish player hacks at the legs of a Greek player and the Greek section of the crowd rise as one. The game resumes and this time it is a Turkish player who sags to the ground. As he writhes the Turkish section rise. Back and forth injuries and indignations are exchanged. Towards the end of the half Rosa persuades her father to shift to another part of the ground, to distance themselves from the supporters of either side. Throughout the trade of insults and abuse, violence, her father's attention clings grimly to events on the field. Rosa's floats to different parts of the ground. It is not what she had imagined. Young men waving their fists at other young men. Once she suggests that they leave but her father doesn't say anything. He's sunk to a place deep within himself, bundled in his suede jacket and scarf, his eyes popping large and unblinking above a grey cropped moustache.

The referee blows up the game ten minutes from the end. Neither side is ahead. Players from both sides remonstrate. They beat their chests. They start to shove at one another. A Turk and a Greek player fall to the ground in an angry exchange, one atop the other. Rosa can see the elbows of the one on top. At this point one section of the crowd becomes enraged and spills on to the ground, quickly followed by the other section. Now spectators are grappling with one another. She pushes her father towards the exit. People are shouting. Shoving from behind. They ride this tide of panic out of the ground.

In the street young men are running in all directions. Her father is confused. He stops. He starts. He looks lost. She pulls him in the direction she wants to go. His breath is hoarse. It is the first time she has seen her father so frightened. She has an idea of what he must have looked like when he was a toddler.

They are hurrying up the street when a line of young men fan across the way to block them. That's their intent. To cut them off. Rosa slows down, clings to her father's side. One of the men jabs his hand in their direction. 'Greek bastards!'

'Se refiere a nosotros?' asks her father. 'No puede ser.'

Now he calls back to them, 'No Greek bastard. What you mean, Greek bastard?'

The other man, thickly moustached, black trousers and a white t-shirt, goes to reply, then stops and looks up the road.

Rosa and her father hear it too. A gear shift, and another gear shift;

then a block of air wallops against her and with a screech of tyres a car slides between her and Roberto and the advancing thugs. It is Ivan. She recognises his lid of brown hair. For once he doesn't look so impassive. She can see his mouth working. He is shouting at them to get in quick. 'Move!' he shouts.

She bundles her father in the back and slides into the front. Before she has slammed the door fists are pounding on the roof. Ivan jams the gearstick forward and reverses. Then they surge forward, her father's feet flying into the air. More screeching of rubber and they hurtle away from the mob.

At some point they are driving in a calmer fashion. At some point Rosa's breathing returns to normal. At some point her father recovers to a sitting position whereupon he leans forward to pat the dishwasher's shoulder.

'Thank you, Ivan.'

And to Rosa, in Spanish, he asks, 'How did he happen to be there?'

She shrugs, as Ivan would, or as a smart alec might say, 'Since when have the rings of Saturn parted from their planet?'

'Luck,' she tells her father.

'Luck,' he nods.

This is how it will go down in history, then.

– 22 –

SHE IS LYING IN A COLD BATH LISTENING TO HER PARENTS TALK IN THE
kitchen. From this distance they sound like two caged birds. Everything
that was good in their life is behind them. Everything that was once
beautiful is fading. They sit lost in this new world, her mother's elbows
on the table, her father's arms dangling at his side. Her mother blames
the humidity for Roberto's depression. In this heat everything goes off.
It is too hot to do anything. It is too hot to think. Rosa sits up in the
cold bath and draws a wave of cold water between her legs and waits
for it to wash back over her groin.

In another hour Ivan will draw up in his old new car. A Holden
with this and that and the other.

'Get in. We'll take her for a spin.'

'Her' refers to the car? Or, is she 'her'? And if so, what is this 'spin'?

Their relationship is developing along the keel of curiosity and explanation.

The 'spin' takes her along Bondi Road. Over the tops of the brick houses she can see the deep lines in the ocean. A white sailboat is bobbing against the immensity of the white and blue world.

They will park at the end of the beach and take the coastal track around the bays as far as the Bronte Cemetery. There, Ivan will conduct his English lesson. Here, where Rosa's beginner's guide is written over the tombstones, they walk up and down, Rosa reciting:

'Gone to a better place . . . On this day . . . Gone from the earth but not from our hearts . . . In everlasting memory . . . a veteran of Crimea . . . a veteran of Crete . . . a veteran of Gallipoli . . . good mate of the Coogee Bowling Club . . . missed by members . . . tragically taken from us . . . mother of, son of, daughter of, father of . . . fondly remembered . . . forever anchored in our hearts.'

– 23 –

ROBERTO'S TRIP TO THE BRONTE CEMETERY BEGINS AT HOME WITH HIM patiently awaiting his death, in a high-back chair, wrapped in blankets that disguise his wasting body, while he watches his favourite film on video. Roberto is too weak to move from his place so Rosa and her mother take it in turns to rewind the video. All hours of the day and night the barking voice of the dance marathon impresario shouts at the walls of the living room: 'Roll up. Roll up and get your number. Around and around we go, and we're only at the beginning, where will it all end, only when two dancers are left standing at the end.' *They Shoot Horses, Don't They?* is part of the home atmosphere, common and regular as the furnishings. On her journey through the house Rosa will stop and pause to note the stumbling progress of Jane Fonda and Michael Sarrazin.

They are still struggling and it seems so pointless given that all the protagonists in the room know the outcome. Sarrazin will comply with Fonda's request and aim a handgun at her temple to end her misery. This is the end they are struggling towards, and so, given Roberto's ambition to starve himself to death, there is a certain empathy. The only time her father shows any sign of life however is to move his lips along with the song sung by the young pregnant drifter:

easy come, easy go..

as it came . . .

let it go . . .

No remorse. No regrets

easy come, easy go.

– 24 –

THERE IS ANOTHER DEPARTURE TO MENTION: HENRY GRAHAM'S.

1929. France.

Each day the tango train from Paris to Deauville passes by the sanitorium. The iron beds are on casters and because it is summer the nurses have rolled the patients outside to sit beneath the rustling leaves of the Dutch and Belgian elms.

The pale TB sufferers are propped up with pillows to keep their blood and phlegm down. But as soon as they hear the approach of the train those who are bedridden inch themselves up their mattresses for a better view. In another minute they will see the figures of the dancers in the carriage windows. The vision at the bottom of the garden comes and goes. And after the last carriage departs and the cows in the pad-dock across the tracks look up, it is easy to question whether what the patients thought they saw actually took place. The cows, the railway line, the paddock. The sick patients who are all dressed in the same striped pyjamas sink back and turn their faces away. Stranded, like fish landed on a river bank, they open their mouths and release blood over the white pillowcases. Soon the cloud in the east will arrive and soon the nurses will wheel them back inside the sanitorium.

One morning there is a signal box failure and the tango train from Paris slows down and stops at the bottom of the garden. If he listens carefully, Henry can hear the orchestra playing. It comes and goes. Comes and goes. He can't quite place the melody. But in the end it's the dancers that trap his attention. It is just movement confined to shadow. It is the broad outline of something he vaguely remembers. The way the women press their cheeks against the cheeks of the men. Two inverted commas. He has seen that before. What is the French expression? *Déjà vu.* Louise and Schmidt, himself and Billy Pohl, and these day trippers from Paris. The cave in the Pacific and the tracks at the bottom of the sanitorium's sunlit garden. It is time and place catching up with itself.

Excited to have made the connection he turns to the young Englishwoman with the blood-splattered collar in the next bed. 'Clare, I want to show you something.' He draws himself up and slides off the bed. The nurses are inside, so Henry leads Clare across the poppy fields to the lawn by the motionless train. Here, the music is louder. They can actually hear individual voices. A woman's laughter. The clatter of trays. The clink of glasses. An English word at least is what they hear — 'exquisite' — as a hand flashes in the window.

By now all the TB sufferers are sitting up in bed to watch Henry and Clare dance in the field by the train.

Once, Clare peeps over her shoulder and smiles shyly back at the congregation. All those still faces, like faces in a painting. She coughs, and before the astonished faces crowding the carriage window her smudged mouth drips blood on to the white collar of the man dancing in his pyjamas. Their faces are so pale. Their eyelids droop. And as the train departs and draws away two black stockinged nurses are seen running across the fields in the direction of the tracks.

Soon the train will trail its smoke and it too will be turned into memory. Or passed on in a letter. And Henry will be remembered by those surviving him. The other patients will jog one another's memory: remember the time the tango train from Paris stopped at the bottom of the garden . . .

- 25 -

THIS WAS THE CROWD I MOVED IN THOSE DAYS. TRAGIC EXILES WHO starved themselves to death; others, inflicted with tuberculosis and dying, out to see themselves off in a final 'three-minute affair'. Insomniacs able to sleepwalk from one part of their life to the other, from the bed of their wife to that of their mistress. Departures of one kind or another . . .

Peter and Jean needed to hear from me that I would be home in time for my father's hip replacement op. My final exam was in the last week of November. By their calculation that would allow me to a week to let my hair down, tie up whatever needed tying up, to pack, and get back to the farm in time for the muster and shearing.

Late at night, as I lay awake, odd details from home shifted into my thoughts. The kitchen cupboards, the paint cracking in places where it had been laid on too thickly. The ceilings, as it now occurred to me, were too shiny, the naked bulb much too bright. The hum of the fridge was too loud. The dogs barking at every ghost climbing over the fence in the night were plain irritating.

At the hostel the telephone rang and rang.

'It's your mother again.' Brice Johns stood in the door, blinking back at me with that news. He couldn't understand why I didn't call back.

Brice was going home for summer and I lay on my bed watching him pack. We'd spent nearly a year together but despite that I couldn't say I really knew Brice; not when I'd spent nearly the same length of time with Rosa. For that matter, I probably felt closer to Louise and Schmidt than I did to my roommate. Years later, someone who had known Brice during this time was to tell me how much Brice hated it when I came back to the room late at night reeking of the restaurant kitchen and Argentinian pot roast. That sounded like Brice. But if he'd had any olfactory sense at all he would have picked up Rosa's Tosca scent. Even as I lay in bed I could smell it on me — and on my pillowcase in the morning.

I sat my final exam. The library closed. Instead of heading back to the farm, as expected, I stepped up my hours at La Chacra. I wanted to make up for lost time. And with Rosa in my orbit I didn't mind being back with Angelo's fatty oven trays, the pots, the food scraps, the soapy grey water; the noise and smells.

December turned out to be a crazy time. Dishes piled high to my shoulder. The waitresses urged me to go faster. Angelo came back yelling for more oven trays. In the weeks leading up to Christmas, one office party after another crammed into La Chacra. Some nights the bandoneon of Troilo was completely drowned out. Other nights there were requests for 'that shit' to be turned up and I'd join the waitresses in the kitchen door to watch some fat-bellied drunk with a loose tie and a Christmas paper hat dance to cries of 'get your gears off'.

One night with drunks falling in and out of one another's arms and Carlos Gardel straining goodnaturedly above it all, Rosa waved her hands to get my attention. As I got closer and saw the phone in her hand, I felt a slowing of the blood in my veins. She shouted into the receiver: 'He's here now, Jean. I pass you over. Ciao for now.' As she handed me the phone Rosa's eye was slightly lidded. I wondered what Jean had told her. For a moment I thought she was going to stand there and watch me talk to my mother. Luckily the noise of someone tumbling to the floor and of glass breaking drew her away.

'Lionel? Lionel, is that you? I can hardly hear you.' My mother's voice sounded small and frail. I could sense the isolation of the farm packed up behind her.

She said, 'I called the hostel. I've left so many messages. God knows. Then it took half an hour for directory to find the restaurant number. Your father thought it was called something else . . . Makara. Or Cracker. You can imagine. I told the woman at directory it was La something . . .'

Jean was ringing to tell me that Peter had put the operation off until late January. So I needn't worry about getting back just yet. But no later than January 20th, or thereabouts. 'Thereabouts' is what I chose to hear.

There was another matter though. She wanted to hear that I would be home for Christmas.

'Meg is flying in from Melbourne especially.'

At that moment Kay ranged in to view. She held a glass above her head.

With all the noise raging around me I had to yell into the receiver: 'Listen, I have to go. This is an impossible time. The restaurant is packed to the gills. I'll call you back. Okay?'

I never did, and the following month my sister wrote me a letter to say she was shocked at how lame our father was, and even more shocked and, frankly, disgusted by my selfishness.

It was easy to be vague and even forgetful. It was rush rush rush.

The week leading up to Christmas frayed our nerves. Meals went to the wrong tables. Angelo snapped at waitresses. The waitresses held back their tears until they made it back to the kitchen. They swore at Angelo. Told each other what a bastard he was. The short-term solution involved words of comfort from Kay; maybe a curt, half-pie apology from Angelo. 'I am sorry. I said I was sorry. Now I have grill for table ten, please.'

Come the end of the night, all was forgiven. After the last of the customers tripped out the door we sat around a table drinking. With a glass in his hand Angelo was back to his charming self. He set about mending fences.

'I am sorry Katrina that I yelled.'

'No. No. It was me. I was so sure they said Steak Argentine.'

And now Rosa would chip in: 'Of course, they are all animals. They come here to get drunk — not to eat. I am sorry, Angelo. But that is the truth.'

These nights the boyfriends of the waitresses were invited in to join us for a late-night drink. By the time everyone left it was too late or else Rosa was too tired to dance.

She waved her hand at the last departing waitress and sat and closed her eyes.

'Pasta, are you still here?'

'Still here,' I said. I was never sure whether she was glad of this or not. She yawned into her hand.

'I shall have to run you home.'

'No. I'm right.'

'Still, it is late.'

The line of her breasts rose and fell as she sighed. She began to push out of her shoes and exercise her toes.

'What did Jean want?' she asked.

'What?'

'Jean. She called the other night . . .'

'Just to say hallo.'

'And?'

'That's it.'

She grunted. She closed her eyes. Just like that my mother was forgotten. She said, 'Be a sweet and rub my feet. I can't feel anything. There is no blood left in my toes. Everything has turned to wood. If I were a tree you would cut me down before I fell down and feed me to the fire.'

I moved a chair closer to her booth so she could lift her swollen feet on to my lap. I massaged her toes, the ball and heel. Rosa purred.

With the arrival of warm summery weather nearly every afternoon I went straight from the Stanley Hope Pool to the restaurant. It was just a short walk through the Public Gardens.

Now I suggested to Rosa, 'Why don't you come swimming with me. It'll give you more energy.'

'So now I need more energy? What do you want . . . that I work myself to an early grave?' She sank further back on to her elbows; her head dropped back so she looked up at the ceiling. Her dress hiked up her thighs. She said, 'Well, maybe you are right. So long as the water is clean.'

Rosa slept in most mornings so it was one or two o'clock before we met at the pool. By then the lunch-hour crowd and the lane swimmers had been and gone.

I liked to get there a bit early in time to see her sweep through the turnstile with head-turning flamboyance. She wore a plum-coloured head scarf, sunglasses, jeans that were a touch too tight, and a shirt tied in a knot over her bare midriff. A downy trail that I found irresistible led from her belly button to the top of her jeans. The first time she caught me staring she pretended to be put out. She yanked off her sunglasses and gave me a sharp look.

'You are looking at my stomach. What is wrong with it?'

'Nothing is wrong with it.'

'So nothing is wrong with it, but you are looking at it.'

There was never any concession to public space. She spoke as loud and as freely as she would in a room with just me and her. I'm sure she enjoyed embarrassing me — this was part of her sport, seeing I was far too aware of the interest of the other pool people, in particular the girls my own age, and all the calculations going on in their heads.

Rosa loved to sunbathe. When she was stripped to her bathing suit every pair of eyes in the pool looked her way. She would lie along the wooden bleachers, and I'd sit upright with a stern look, like the palace guard; the guys couldn't stop looking at her crotch, at the hemline that struggled to contain her pubic hair. Let's say she attracted a lot of interest.

This afternoon it is a guy older than myself, in his late twenties I'd say, well tanned, a toned upper body. His chest is greasy with oil. Sunglasses are pushed up against his forehead. This is how it works. He stops to ask me the time — they all do that — and all the while staring at Rosa's crotch. Rosa has on her sunglasses so she can see what is going on. He doesn't know this of course. He is the Lone Ranger and I am Tonto. I tell him the time and we move on to the next phase. He whips out a pack of cigarettes. He asks me if I want a smoke. And as he makes this offer he thinks he might as well join us and sits himself down, at which point Rosa sits up, pushes back her sunglasses and gives the man a frosty look.

'Lionel, do you know this man?'

'No, I don't,' I answer.

'So if he is not an acquaintance why is he sitting with us?'

It was like she'd aimed a revolver at the side of his head. The Lone Ranger holds up his hands in mock surrender, picks up his towel and moves his oily body along.

196

The Lone Ranger's artlessness stayed with me. What else was he to do, though? I thought a good deal about this. It seemed to me that this was where dance and its guiding rituals came in handy. There was a procedure to follow, rails to hold on to.

Another time I arrive at the pool to find Rosa already there. Now I note the second surprise. She is standing at the far end of the pool with someone I've never seen before. For all I know it might be someone she just happened to run across. Or else — and this is more likely — it is another Lone Ranger climbed down off his horse. The two of them are smoking. I guess he must have asked Rosa if she wanted a cigarette and this time she must have found a reason to accept. She's the one doing the talking. The man seems pleased to have her company. His arms are folded. A cheesy smile says he can't believe his luck. About now he looks up and sees me, and that alerts Rosa. She glances back and this time there is no recognition at all. I might as well be a complete stranger. I have to pretend that I've left something back at the counter; I go around the other side of the pool to the men's changing shed. When I come out the Lone Ranger was gone.

I didn't see the man again. Rosa never mentioned him and I didn't ask, but for a horrible split second it was as though we had already passed out of one another's life. These incidents aren't so much about Rosa. They are about me. They are about my fierce devotion to Rosa. 'Your jealousy,' Rosa would say, her head bobbing with its smile. Teasing me. Stabbing her fingers into my ribs. But when she rested her head on my leg and closed her eyes this was happiness. So were our discussions when for a rare moment I was able to forget her physical attractions and think about what she was actually saying. There was always something to decide. An issue to resolve.

One night she saw a swastika tattooed over the forearm of a man paying for his dinner. It was as he was writing out a cheque that his shirtsleeve happened to ride up his arm and that's when she saw the swastika. She wanted to say something; she felt the need to make him account for it, to get him to explain why he had done such a thoughtless thing. Yet everything else about the man seemed in conflict with the crudeness of the tattoo. He had complimented her on a fine meal — the finest, he said, that he'd had in some time. He'd been complimentary to a new waitress. The moment when Rosa might have spoken up came and went. Afterwards, to upbraid herself for her failure of nerve, she ripped up his cheque.

At the pool she asked me, 'What would you have done?'

'I think I would have said something.'

'You would have?'

She was quick and sharp with that.

'Yes, I would have. I think.'

She squinted across at the bleachers on the other side of the pool.

'It is better to be honest with one's feelings, yes?'

'Yes,' I said.

Rosa continued to squint.

'You don't seem so sure,' I said.

'That is because I am not so sure.'

I waited for her to elaborate. Perhaps it was too hard, because this speculative talk ended, for the moment anyhow, with her grunting and the more down-to-earth matter of her arranging my leg to rest her head. Across the pool, on the bleachers, three girls my own age, sitting in a wet line, caught my eye. They blushed and looked away. Rosa reached down and waggled my foot.

'Say something,' she said.

'I'm thinking.'

I was back to considering the diner with the swastika. I like to think I would have said something; in an ideal world we always know what to say and when. But then I also knew that my nerve had failed me when Jean rung up. I knew I wasn't going back to the farm.

'Hello?' said the voice on my lap.

'I'm still thinking,' I said.

She said, 'I think your brain must have more loops in it than mine. I have a thought and you are you are still circling the track. I have another thought and still you are going around and around . . .'

'Sorry.'

'Don't be sorry. I will tell you about Billy Pohl instead.'

$$- 26 -$$

Billy still holds on to the letter Louise wrote him with her world-record-breaking claim that she had fallen in love inside three minutes. About the same length of time that a milkman making deliveries in the early hours comes into hearing range and departs again.

Whenever Billy tucks in his shirt and tightens his belt he can feel the letter in his shirt pocket press against his heart.

In a moment though he will feel the ample breast of Margaret Spooner. There she is, wriggling her hips in spite of herself, in a bevy of rural beauties lining the district hall. Billy moves towards her. He is like a ship coming into port, the sea of people on the dance floor clearing between them, the landscape spreading out beyond that original point of contact, which for Margaret was a certain come-hither look combined with rural bashfulness. At his approach Margaret, in the approved fashion, drops her eyes, looks away, looks back, sets her mouth, and Billy notices, the mark of lipstick smudged against her teeth. She must have nibbled her lip. So she's nervy like himself. That's good. A woman too confident is hopeless to dance with. The deft touch is lost. You might as well piss into the wind. What happens is this. You find yourself stacking bricks, laying them down, picking them up, and setting them down again as you make your way from one corner of the dance floor to the next.

Margaret's not bad on the dance floor, though. Lighter than he thought would be the case. He's moving into his work now. And at some point she whispers, 'Where did you learn to dance like that, Billy Pohl?'

She is blushing like a new tomato. Must have been when his thigh brushed the inside of hers.

Love is already ripening its seed in the Tautapere Hall. To think he wasn't even going to come to the dance!

Still, what you do on your own accord is never what you recommend for another, especially when it is your daughter.

It's 1958, and a youth with an oil slick and a duck wave for a haircut, all muscle inside a white t-shirt, has dropped around to the house in his loud car this Saturday night to pick up Billy and Margaret's youngest daughter, Sharee. One peep from behind the kitchen curtain and Billy has an urge to part with the facts of life. 'Don Juan out there,' he starts to say, but that brings him a cold stare. He's being sarky. Okay, he'll try again. 'Sharee, I'm going to tell you something that I've never told your mother. It is possible for you to fall in love in the course of one dance, three minutes flat.' The confused young face peeps out from her fringe of brown hair. 'Well, that's all, Sharee. Go out and enjoy yourself. Just remember what I said about the three-minute affair.'

'Strange,' says his daughter. 'You're strange.'

With a father's heart Billy stands at the window as his daughter walks up the path to the street, batting her mother's eyes, spreading her wings, ready to enact history and claim her future.

Louise still thinks of Billy, after all this time. She has lived more years now than the number remaining to her. Alone in her Almagro flat, the mind is sorting and compiling. It focuses and clears out extraneous matter. There is Schmidt, there are the city rooftops of Buenos Aires; there is her former life, increasingly more vivid and clearcut these days — Little River, the noise that a seagull makes dropping a shellfish on to an iron roof, the smell of the smoke-filled nights in Little River's main street, the inflamed face of the station master, and Billy Pohl, his slouching figure passing the picket fence, the blue-black of his beard and his silences as he dries his clothes on the drying rack.

She tries to picture him now.

There isn't really anyone remotely like him in Buenos Aires. But there are bits and pieces to graft on to a memory. The gentle stomach sag of the retired schoolteacher who visits the shop to pick up strings for his guitar. Or the back view of the violinmaker, his working shoulders oddly reminiscent of Billy sitting on the step outside sorting his flounder net. Or the splayed legs of the man sitting next to her on the bus this morning, his tobaccoey smell. When she rose to her feet to get past him for her stop he had looked up with surprise, no doubt wondering why this woman was smiling down at him.

Old conversations drift back to her.

'Tonight, I'm going to dance your legs off.'

'Here, Louise, throw a stone in to the still water and watch the ripples fan out.'

The first is a boast of Billy Pohl's. The second a directive from Paul Schmidt.

– 27 –

Buenos Aires. 1968.

In a city divided by rivers of traffic and without a coastline there is no place to walk free of your life. The skinny streets fold back to vast avenues, all choked with traffic and noise. The effect is pulverising to the senses.

It is the same thing every day. It never stops. When Billy Pohl wakes up in the Hotel Chile the first thing he hears is the sound of traffic thundering by beneath his window. The street cleaners lead the parade. Then come the buses with their heavy gear work as they chop down for the corner his hotel sits on. How and when did the world become such a noisy place? He glances up at the ceiling, wondering what in God's name brought him here in the first place. Louise. Unfinished business. He smiles back at the young face in his memory — then reaches for his teeth sitting in the glass of water on the bedside vanity. Pulls on his clothes. Closes the cage door on the lift and descends to the street where he walks into a headwind of fumes and noise, heading for the nearby café with the varnished pastries in the window.

He always looks for a table on its own; preferably in a corner where he can mutter his request up through his hand to the waitress. He hates it when the others in the café lift their nosy heads out of their newspapers, the way their ears prick. The slow thoughtful stir of their teaspoons. Billy hating his foreignness. Hating to be singled out — especially whenever the waitress departs from the established form. She must know what he wants by now. He's been here four mornings in a row and each time he's asked for exactly the same thing. Why does she have to spray him with incomprehensible language and ask him these other things? Tostada, Señor? '*See. See.* Whatever.' He waves her away. Yesterday he found he'd ordered an omelette which he ate without complaint. But he drew the line at black coffee. He sat upright and sternly folded his arms until the waitress noted his wounded face.

'Si, Señor?'

Billy pointed at a glass of latte on another table. He wanted one like that.

'Si, Señor.'

Today he is in a hurry. In another thirty minutes or so he will take a taxi out to the cemetery at Chacarita where after a series of blunders he will find his way to the door of the English-speaking director. The director will look up Louise's details and on a map of the *cementerio* show Billy the way to her grave.

Years later, when I met the director, at first he didn't remember Billy at all. Then I thought to add a detail that had struck Rosa when Billy showed up at her father's music store.

'He was possibly wearing a green and white blazer with a pennant?'

Billy's best blazer was his Riverton Bowling Club one. Rosa remembered the ribbons and pennants embossed with the years of triumph. Billy told her, 'This one for the Club Pairs; that one for the Fours I skippered from 1952 to '63.'

The director, by now well advanced in years himself, began to slowly nod.

'Ah, the lawn bowler.' The word 'lawn' forced his mouth wider to a view of a tooth in the corner of his jaw that was out of alignment with the others. He stood up behind his desk and walked to the window with the sweeping view of the *calles* and their extraordinary tombs. He folded his hands behind his back. Yes, he remembered. He had personally escorted the old man to Louise's grave.

It was a hot day and a bit of a struggle for Billy. They stopped at a bench within view of the gallerias for Billy to sit and get his breath back. Billy mopped his face with his handkerchief, the director tapping his fingers on the seat, impatient to get back to the office. Billy, on the other hand, was content to sit and gaze at the huge walls of coffins. 'By golly, don't they look like office filing cabinets?' the director remembers him saying. The unexpected image of filing cabinets prompted him to ask about Billy's work, and without missing a beat Billy answered:

'Rates office. Invercargill City Council.'

Within another three days he would be slotted into galleria 21 with a bus driver, a piano teacher and a dress-maker for neighbours.

The final moment came as he left the same café he always went to for breakfast. The usual waitress Billy relied on to make himself understood wasn't on that day. A new woman was in her place. One who shouted so the whole café could hear — a torrent of Spanish that lifted heads out of newspapers. Billy became more and more flustered. He wanted coffee. A cup of coffee. Café. *Café?* White. No sugar. *No sooker.*

The whole bloody world understands that.

'N'entiendo, Señor.'

She continued to stand there looking down at him, pencil and pad at the ready.

'Y quieres algo a comer?'

Billy gave up at that point. He pushed his chair out, grabbed his hat and left. He was wild with frustration. Tired of foreigners. Tired of the battle to make himself understood. Without looking he waded into the traffic of Avenida de Mayo. Taxis honked. Billy waved back contemptuously. Cars weaved. A bus bore down on him. He had to move quickly to get out of its way; then there were another two lanes, a line of taxis to beat. He had nearly made it to the other side when an oncoming car braked heavily. Billy froze: the screech of brakes and the slow motion of the car were strangely at odds with each other. He made it up on to the sidewalk. Out of breath he grabbed at his collar. He managed to loosen it but his chest still felt tight. It felt like every loose end in him had suddenly been pulled on. By golly. He was going to have to sit down on the sidewalk. He was going to have to sit down in front of all these people. He would have to do it — even if it meant the population stepping over him.

The desk clerk from the Hotel Chile saw the commotion through the glass doors. The first time he hadn't taken much notice. The second time he looked up and saw the green bowling club blazer and rushed outside; by this time Billy was dead. The hotel clerk knelt by Billy and looked up at the ring of people. The mystery of Billy was on each of their faces. Death drew studied lines in their expressions. It occurred to the clerk that he was the last person to whom Billy had spoken to. 'Ola, Martin, I'm just going out to get some breakfast.'

I prefer not to leave Billy Pohl on the sidewalk like something fallen out of the sky. I prefer to see him as Rosa did when Billy came to the family apartment smelling violently of aftershave, sporting a red rash over his neck, and in his bowler's blazer sitting on the same couch as Rosa's grandmother with all that overlapping experience between them, and neither able to understand a word of the other.

– 28 –

NOTHING IS EVER QUITE AS YOU EXPECT OR HOPE IT WILL BE. IN LOUISE'S old neighbourhood of Almagro a street has been named after her beloved Troilo, but there the association ends. Some forward-thinking city planner on his way up in 1950-something, to judge by the surrounding boxy architecture, has seen fit in the name of modernity to seal the cobbled road. Progress takes many shapes, and happily the tarseal is coming apart and in patches an authentic scrap of Troilo's cobbled past is revealed.

Perhaps Troilo stood here? Or over there? You take another step to assert the possibility. You glance around, speculating. That view of the old plaster façade, the last in the street, that too can be added to Troilo's and Louise's neighbourhood.

The combustive roar you hear is the traffic streaming down Corrientes. Several blocks down from Troilo a splashy new shopping mall, all glancing window and light, takes the Gardel name. The original market of Gardel's youth and this new air-conditioned consumer's palace are, so I'm told, approximately the same place. A uniformed guard said as much when I went in to use the flashy toilets. Around the corner from the shopping mall a new statue of a Gardel smiled back at yet another note-taker.

Richer pickings are to be had at the corner of Corrientes and Sanchez de Bustamante, where, the approximate whereabouts of Gardel's backyard has been preserved. A clumsily hand-painted sign reads — Carlos Gardel Quinta. If you stop to listen you will hear a recording of a songbird from an electronic device attached unobtrusively to one of the trees.

Music? It remains constant. Gardel and Troilo and Goyeneche. The big three still command huge sections of any music store; it's almost as if they haven't died. You can buy their painted portraits and photos at the fleamarket on Plaza Dorrega. There, you can drop a coin into the dancer's hat. And on the other side of the square a thirteen-year-old boy singer is introduced to the crowd as the 'young Gardel'.

One drizzly midweek night, marooned on a downtown island in the vast Avenida de Julio with more than a dozen lanes of traffic passing in both directions, I happened to look up Avenida Cordoba and, directly ahead, blinking in hideously green neon was this:

LA CHACRA

In the restaurant window four sheep carcasses were being spit-roasted in the manner of a beach barbecue. A large steer clothed in brown woolly-eyed innocence stood in the entranceway. A line of tables with starched white cloths marched back to swing doors at the rear. After staring in the window, I walked back to the traffic island where for some time, oblivious to the traffic if such a thing can be imagined in Buenos Aires, I stood looking back at the neon of La Chacra, mildly exhilarated to have arrived at the source.

In every other respect the city I find myself in is different from the one in which Louise lived. Buenos Aires has spread to the pampas; swallowed them whole. There is the traffic, of course. God knows, it never stops, except intermittently beneath my hotel window and then only for an hour between five and six in the morning. The yellow taxis are so numerous you could walk across their tops from one end of the city to the other. The *milongas* are hot, breathless places where the young dance in sneakers and the elderly throw away their crutches. In Buenos Aires, at least, the dance floor remains the spring of youth.

Turning to the attractions of my own guidebook, the location of Troilo's *danzarín* turns out to be a muddy *dique* on the Buenos Aires waterfront. At first it's hard to see what could have inspired such a stirring melody. There is the climbing white backdrop of the city. There are the breakwaters; a lone tree, like the last of its kind, perches on the end of one. You pass the glassed-in restaurant setting of the Buenos Aires yacht club. Then you come across the pier where Louise and Schmidt used to rendezvous, and there you find the whole drama of arrival and departure — the moment of giddy anticipation and the flat sadness because of its passing and that, I suspect, is the spirit of the man who wrote Rosa's favourite song.

On the day I visited, fishermen lined the pier, their heads and shoulders drooping over the top rail. Now and then a fish rose from the muddy water in a silvery flash. I walked on to the end of the pier. It's easy to see why Schmidt hated meeting Louise here. It's the only place in Buenos Aires, at ground level, at least, where you are aware of the horizon. And the horizon is there to remind us of what we seek and what we have left behind. It is the dividing line of experience. While she waited for Schmidt to show up I like to think of Louise drawing up her own list. On the deficit side: the want of a happy domestic life with Schmidt, children, grandchildren. And the continuation of one's own story that progeny carry within them. On the other side of the score sheet, romance.

Louise weathered revolution and a war in which her host country sided with the enemy. At least this time Schmidt's name was less of a liability. She saw the rise of Perón and his wife, Evita. I imagine Louise kept her political leanings to herself. I have a sense of her harbouring conservative tendencies, possibly finding some things to admire in Perón while disdaining his efforts at ceaseless self-promotion. But this is just wild speculation, something to toss about in my head while my hand rakes the peanut bowl in the bar at the top of Honduras — remember that fork in the road with its diminishing point through the trees.

There was talk of another coup when I visited Buenos Aires. People shrugged. It is possible. Maybe. Maybe not. They moved their fingers through the baskets of peanuts. The talk might as well have concerned the weather. It will rain. It will shine. If you just sit patiently it is like nothing ever happened.

Small schoolchildren in their white smocks and looking like miniature chemists floated by the bar window. Rain had started to fall. A dog walker slipped on a cobblestone. The melancholy beer drinkers stared at their last mouthful sitting at the bottom of their glass.

I sat gazing out the window at the fork in the road. The sooty branches of the jacarandas probed the sky and at a distant point appeared to provide an arc across Honduras. The defiant faces of the cart boys employed to pick up dogshit from the city streets looked in the window at two girls their own age peering at the screen of a laptop — youth in its various guises, each thinking itself unique and like the world has never seen. I took another sip of beer. My attention floated back to the apartment building at the top of Honduras and I noted how it fronted on to different streets. I thought about the lives of Señora Schmidt and Louise, and how they had backed on to each other — neither particularly aware of the other except as a distraction or background noise. Pleasantries exchanged in the hall or in the lift; in my beery state I was starting to see them as two butterfly wings attached to the corpus of Schmidt. He needed both to fly.

On my last day there I hadn't quite found what I hoped to. In a hairbrained moment I decided to knock on the door of Louise's old apartment. A plainly flustered woman answered and handed me a crying baby. She mistook me for the father returned at last to relieve her of her babysitting duties. Through broken Spanish and sign language I managed to persuade her to let me in and roam like a city health inspector. I looked quickly and felt no connection at all; disappointed, I turned to thank the poor, confused woman. I signed off with a ludicrous semi-military salute, hurried for the stairs; across the courtyard a horde of grubby-faced porteño children howled at my back — 'amigo! amigo! señor! señor!'

– 29 –

ONE AFTERNOON AT THE POOL I TELL ROSA I HAVE A SURPRISE TO
show her.

She says, 'I also have some news. But yours first.'

Her head turns for the pool clock. She mutters something about
the restaurant. She has to get more wine in. She's promised Angelo to
pick up a box of ice lettuce. As usual she is in a hurry.

Now I have to tell her that the 'surprise' is a short drive away.

'No. It is impossible. It can wait for tomorrow.'

'It'll take ten minutes. You can set your watch by it if you don't
believe me.'

'And Angelo will shoot me if I don't have his things . . .'

'Ten minutes. What's ten minutes?'

'It depends what time of the day we are talking about . . .'

'Please. Rosa.' I've been busting with the surprise since she got to the pool.

'Okay. But I will tell Angelo that it is your fault that he is late with his lettuce. You have no idea. He treats me like I am his servant. Rosa get this. Rosa, I need more this, that.'

Twenty minutes later, in another part of town to which she is unaccustomed, a light industrial area studded with old turn-of-the century villas, many in disrepair and some derelict, I lead her up a flight of wooden steps. The queasy-making smell of wax from the downstairs candlemaker turns her head. Her grip on my arm tightens. 'What is this . . .? What have you brought me to?'

To add to the 'surprise' I have blindfolded her with her scarf. 'It is childish of course. You see what I do for you. You and Angelo. I do these things and for what . . .?'

'We're nearly there,' I tell her.

She reaches up to pull at the blindfold.

'This is ridiculous.' Then she asks, 'Can anyone see us?'

'Just those people crammed in the window,' I tell her and immediately she stops and looks blindly about.

'Where? Where? Lionel, take off this stupid . . .'

But we've arrived. I turn the key and push the door open. I stand aside for Rosa. It's been fun up to now. Here's the part I'm unsure about.

I untie the blindfold and there's a moment of adjustment where she stays put in the doorway, at this threshold, blinking, braced for surprise with held breath. So far she's not surprised. But what she sees hasn't

216

been expected either. She is somewhere in between — apprehensive is the word I'm after. The white-painted walls of the interior draw her in. Now she sees my denim jacket hanging off the back of a kitchen chair. The chair had come with the flat. I wouldn't have been able to afford it otherwise. She notes my bookshelves, such as they are — two pieces of timber I flogged from a Burke's bin — and the bricks they rest on. The shelves are the most colourful item in the room. But I'm also proud of the tasteful combination of creamy colours and the broadleaf green of the few pot plants I have been able to afford. I hope she has noticed this. One by one Rosa takes in these details, this spectacular evidence of my new, independent life — away from the farm, away from the schoolish hostel with its warden and curfew hour. As her eye prowls the exhibit I watch her mentally ticking various boxes. Knowing I'd be leading her here this afternoon I scrubbed it clean. That's the cleansing fluid, Pine-something, that her nose has just picked up. With Rosa here the Pine feels like a character reference. But these are things on their own. It's the overall response that she is fishing for. She isn't sure what to say or how to react.

Now she stands at the window to gather her thoughts. The view isn't much. A few cars are parked in the street below. The pitched and flat rooftops fall away. There is the flattening effect of grey and muggy skies.

'You were right,' she says at last. 'This is a surprise.'

But when she says this it doesn't sound like a surprise. She doesn't sound surprised, either. If anything she sounds depressed. The whole glorious moment is set to deflate. She unfolds her arms; folds them again. Now she drops them at her side.

'Lionel,' she begins.

I know what she is about to say. I know it by the tone what's coming and I don't want to hear it. I do not want to hear it said that I've overstepped the mark.

'I have tea. Would you like a cup of tea?'

She looks around the room.

'There is nowhere to sit.'

'You can sit on the bed if you like.'

'I don't see a bed. I see a mattress on the floor.'

'That's the bed.'

'And I'm a 36-year-old woman.'

I didn't anticipate this. I had thought she would be pleased. I'd have thought she'd seen what I had in mind; that this is our place. Somewhere that isn't so public. Somewhere that isn't the restaurant or the pool. She says, 'I don't see any music. A home without music is a person without a soul.'

'I have music.'

In fact this was supposed to be my next surprise. I've made copies of the tapes from the restaurant. I put on a favourite of Rosa's — Goyeneche singing 'Vuelvo al Sur' and hold out my arms. She looks away to the window but gradually the song catches her and brings her back and she can't resist. We dance *milonga* style, cheek to cheek.

There is a place in Goyeneche's song where he stops singing to declaim each word, releasing each one syllable by syllable. The first time I heard 'Vuelvo al Sur' I pictured Dean Martin with a drink in his hand, half-remembering, half-forgetting, an amiable TV drunk grinning and willing sympathy from me, Meg, Peter and Jean lined up on the couch at home. The difference here is that Goyeneche's pause is not forgetfulness. It is more deliberate than that. It is to enable what will happen to happen. A *corte*. However with Rosa I find myself rocking back and forth in a kind of stasis. She smiles and waits. At last, suppressing a giggle, she releases herself.

The moment in which to push forward in to a new situation has been and gone. Now she looks at her watch.

'Now look. Despite what you said, despite what you promised me, you have made me late. Angelo will hate me. He will revile me for his lettuces.'

She's already on her way. I call after her, 'Wait. You said you had a surprise for me.'

'Oh, that.'

She looks vaguely around the room. She thinks for a moment more.

'Yes, well, that can wait. There has been enough surprise for one day.'

Angelo was first to notice the impact of the bedsit on my finances. He observed me eating more when I came in to start my shift, binge eating and picking over the scraps on plates.

'First I give you pasta, then you want a steak. This is not a normal appetite, my friend. Perhaps you are pregnant?'

I looked up from the steak he'd just cooked me.

'Just a joke, my friend.'

It amazed me what I had to spend just to stay alive. Nearly everything I earned from the restaurant went towards the rent, the rest on milk, tea, bread and a few staple items. At the end of the week I had nothing to show for my labour at La Chacra.

I asked Rosa if I could extend my hours. And with a hint of bravado I said, 'Maybe I should look around for a second job. What do you think?'

We were on our way to the markets. Rosa was driving. She took her time to answer, pursing her lips while she thought about the possibilities.

'Maybe,' she said, and there the matter sat as we slowed for the next set of lights. In the car, especially in traffic, Rosa needed to devote herself fully to the road. After a pause she said, 'If it is money you need then maybe I can help. Well, I am thinking Ivan actually. Maybe he can help.'

Ivan's name hadn't been mentioned in weeks, not since her stories at the pool of Roberto starving himself to death before the dance video. Her father's decline had provided Ivan with his moment of reckoning. A *corte* out in the real world. He'd stepped up to the mark at the Almagro Steak House and grown into the chef's position.

In delicate silence Rosa spoke softly but firmly.

'That was my news. Remember?' And then, more brightly as if this was glad tidings I could share in too, 'Well,' she said, 'Ivan is coming back.'

'Why is he?' I blurted.

'What do you mean "Why is he?"'

The car behind tooted.

'The lights are green,' I said.

'I can see. I know what green is.'

She graunched through the gear changes. At last, in top gear, we settled back.

'Pasta,' she said gently. 'Have you forgotten. Ivan is my husband. I am married to him.'

'I know what a husband is,' I said.

'Now you are angry.'

'I am surprised.'

'No,' she said. 'You're angry.'

I didn't want to argue over the fine point of exactly how I felt. Though I don't think it was anger. Rosa's calmly delivered news left me temporarily dazed. I'd given up thinking about Ivan months ago. Even at the pool when I listened to Rosa's account of Ivan's safe pair of hands guiding the Almagro through the period of her father's decline, Ivan's name seemed safely in the past. Not once had I heard her mention or even hint at Ivan coming back into her life. But then I was blind to certain coincidences that only years later would take on greater definition, like a shape emerging from a fog. Ivan was the missing element. We were poised to enter that marginalised space that Schmidt and his 'faithful shop assistant' had occupied.

– 30 –

Around this time the newspapers carried a story on a huge meteorite hurtling Earth's way. They were full of scientific speculation and talk of instant climatic changes, and the rapid extinction of us all that would follow. At La Chacra, at the end of the shift when we sat around drinking and talking, we thought about what we might do. Crouch under a table or stand in a doorway or just stay where we were and defiantly stir our teabags. On impact, we were told, the meteorite would shatter into a million fragments. During these discussions I thought of Ivan.

Two days before he was due to fly in, Rosa asked me to spend a few hours at her house to help put things back the way Ivan was used to.

This was the first time I had been to Rosa's place. Nothing about it seemed to fit the person. The choice of where she lived seemed no more than incidental.

Rosa's house was one in a line of ordinary weatherboard houses. Her section however stood out, though for all the wrong reasons. The grass ran to clay patches. The flowerbeds were overgrown with weeds. And this was the house of somebody whose day was ruined if she spotted a crumb on the floor of the restaurant!

The anonyminity continued inside. I had expected to find more things from her life in Buenos Aires or Sydney. There was her grandfather's record collection. She dug out some of Louise's records from the pile, old jacket covers of Gardel and Solsa, their colours washed out. You saw the passing effect of time. Their complexions were too rosy and creamy. They were faded remnants of what they had been, like pressed flowers. I looked up at the walls — there were no pictures. Their starkness gave prominence to a photo portrait of Troilo with his pallbearer's face, his small chinless mouth. He looked like a man accused of some heinous crime and unable to defend himself. There was one other artefact of note. On top of a speaker stood a section of glass from the shop window in the chic neighbourhood of Palermo: *Schmidt: música y importador, Buenos Aires, 1926.*

Rosa seemed to read my thoughts.

'It is a house. Not a home. But if it's a home you wish then I have photographs.'

She went into another room and came back with an armful of albums. The green fabric cover was worn through to pale bone-coloured paper. She opened this album and there was the pink villa, with its black-shuttered windows. She turned the page and 'introduced' me to her grandmother, a matriarchal figure who at a glance you know as one of those women who will accept certain losses in order to preserve the appearance of the whole, her heart aching as she sets the splendid table beneath an outside garden trellis on the occasion of Schmidt's sixty-fifth birthday.

We quickly thumbed through the other albums with Rosa pulling faces at her younger self, insisting on defects when none were obvious. Her eyes are too wide apart, her hair a mess — or this for example, of the photo taken of her dancing in Hyde Park on Australia Day: 'Look how thin I am. Too thin. I am dying.' At the same time, secretly, and not so secretly proud of her beauty.

We arrived at the wedding photos. Rosa in white. Ivan, delighted with the outcome. Tucked inside a brown hire suit, legs astride, feet planted firmly. The tired and worn-out woman beside him is Maria, Rosa's mum.

The tour ended, Rosa's gathered up the albums and we set to work. Really there wasn't much to do. A huge TV had to be hauled back from its place of exile in a spare room at the back of the house. At one point I managed a quick glimpse into Rosa's bedroom. There was just time to see a bedpost and a floor rug before Rosa closed the door.

But here was the real reason for getting me over. In the hall she held a stepladder while I reached through the ceiling trapdoor. Rosa directed from below. 'The cartons should be to the left . . .' As I brought the first one down I saw a number of small moulded dogs on wooden stands. These were trophies for dog grooming Ivan had won in competitions across New South Wales and Victoria. That's where he had been these past months; with his dog grooming franchise and competing for trophies.

On Christmas Eve a small gift wrapped in Christmas paper waited for me on the kitchen bench. There was a note attached warning me to 'please unwrap with care'. Inside I found a music score, a very old one which before Rosa was to tell me I guessed right away had belonged either to Schmidt or Louise. It was Troilo's 'Danzarin'.

This was incredibly generous. I knew how important it was to her, this piece of music connecting her to her grandfather and to Louise. It was an heirloom she had gifted to me.

She had also arranged presents for the rest of the staff. At the end of the night Kay and the other waitresses lined up to thank Rosa for their bottle of wine and box of Turkish Delight. Besides myself, Angelo was the only other staff member singled out for a special gift. His was a chef's apron with the word *maestro* embroidered in green stitching. He added something in Spanish that ended with the pleasant-sounding *maestro,* and something else more melting, so that for a brief flashing moment Rosa looked young and bashful. I wanted to know what Angelo had said so I could repeat it at the first opportune moment alone with her.

Champagne was poured. Toasts were made to Rosa and La Chacra, to its eternal success. Angelo emptied his glass with a single gulp. He refilled it. His face glowing, he offered second and third toasts.

The boyfriends trickled in. Bulging in their muscle shirts. Big Polynesian boys who sang in their church choir, drank orange juice and worked on the doors of various pubs and clubs around town. The waitresses perched on their knees. They were unusually relaxed.

Released from their chores they turned in to swans and preened their feathers. I imagined the wild sex they were in for later and I thought with envy how easy and uncomplicated it was for them. At the end of the night I would return to my bedsit; Rosa would leave for home where Ivan, newly returned, just hours earlier as it happened, was probably waiting up for her.

Among the waitresses that night I noticed a new attention to the music. For the very first time they seemed to actually listen to Gardel and Goyeneche, like birds who up to this moment had shown no special regard for the particular sky they'd flown in. Now as they stood their hair flowed past their shoulders. They moved dreamily with their painted fingernails hanging at their sides, their shoulders twisting, some with a look of rapture that I thought would match their face asleep on the pillow. Really they had no idea how to dance.

At a certain point when the soft Ballada came on, Rosa and I looked for one another. Instincts. Instincts. What powerful magnets they are. We moved to the middle of the floor as we would have at the end of a normal evening shift after the last waitress had gone, and we began to dance. As usual I felt the rough edges fall off me. I became emboldened. Everything we tried seemed to come off. I didn't notice the waitresses making space for us. I didn't notice that we had an audience until the song finished and the waitresses applauded and wolf-whistled. 'Way to go, Lionel. Way to go.' The waitresses pressed around. 'My God, where did you learn to do that? That's amazing.' I beamed back at the bank of smiling faces. To their rear, Kay and Angelo stood apart with looks of judgment that went beyond what they had just witnessed to juggling another question — how it had come to pass in the first place? My eyes met Kay's. She dropped her gaze and reached for her glass. I watched her swallow. Angelo's smile was more smug and direct; he wanted me to know that he wasn't fooled.

Now the waitresses wanted to see us dance again, so we danced to Piazolla's 'Oblivion', a quiet, trembling melody respectful of the late hour. We danced with cheeks pressed together, our eyelids closed.

The music ended. We rocked in place a few extra seconds then parted. There was a delayed response from the audience this time, a gap in proceedings for all kinds of suspicion to wash about. Then as Rosa and I moved to an arm's length apart, the faces relaxed. I detected a sigh of relief around the room. It was only a dance, after all.

- 31 -

CHRISTMAS DAY. AS SOON AS I WOKE I THOUGHT, IVAN'S BACK. RIGHT NOW he is in bed with Rosa. It wasn't just depressing. It completely immobilised me. Yet as I lay on my mattress it also occurred to me that I knew Rosa as Ivan must know her. I knew her as a husband did. Her touch. The feel and taste of her mouth. The amazing stillness of her sleep. Her way of lying on her back in layers and clouds of smoke, her words coming unstuck from the back of her throat as she floated them up at the ceiling. To that extent Ivan and I had something in common. We shared an intimacy with Rosa. It didn't occur to me that it might be a different intimacy or that intimacy, like dancing, can be a variable experience.

I got up and dressed. I stood at the window for a while then went out to the kitchen, switched on the jug and returned to the window. This was the first Christmas I'd spent away from my family; away from the farm.

This was also the time that Louise used to dread. Holiday time. Schmidt's family time. Stuck in her flat, in a nowhere state of mind, changing records on her RCA Victor, watching the light come and go in the window.

I reread the short letter from Jean asking me to call home on Christmas Day. They hadn't heard from me in such a while. Meg was already there. She had come home a week earlier than expected for some reason. My big sister wanted to hear from me. The letter ended: 'PS. Reverse the charges.'

I thought of them at home, grouped around the long dining table. I imagined the Wheelers would be over for the dinner, Chrissie in one of her soft woolly tops, my father swaying on his one good leg, uncorking bottles, making sure everyone was happy, that everyone's spirit was turned up to his own. I found myself back at the window, smiling down at an empty street, a cup of tea in my hand. There was no milk. And no place open to go and get some.

I didn't own a TV or a radio. But I did have my tape deck. I put on Troilo and tried to follow the notes on the score of 'Danzarin'. But after a while this was too much like homework; I put it to one side and stretched out on the mattress to wait for Rosa. I was sure she would turn up. Hour after hour my optimism remained undimmed. Any moment now I would hear her on the steps outside.

Two deadly boring days dragged by before there was a knock on the door. I sprang up, all my nerve endings jangling. At last. I pulled on a t-shirt and hurried to the back door. But it wasn't Rosa. It was a younger woman in jeans and brown hair, wearing stylish dark tortoise-patterned sunglasses. She was someone I knew I was supposed to recognise. But for the moment I stood there and said nothing. Then she moved her sunglasses back.

'Meg!'

My sister was reserved at first. She was angry with me. Fancy me not coming home to see her!

She marched through the kitchen, full of entitlement. In the middle of the room she stopped and looked around. The morning's bowl of cereal was still on the floor next to my mattress. She parked her gaze there for a moment. Then she walked to the window and unlatched it. She pulled back one of the curtains to even the window space up.

'So this is how you live?'

She was staring down at my mattress.

I said half apologetically, 'I haven't had much time to get stuff in. Do you want a cup of tea?'

'In here? No. I'll take you somewhere. Big sister's treat. Not that you deserve it.'

I noticed she didn't have any bags.

'Everything is at the airport. I just wanted to check in with you before I flew out. I don't know when I'll be back, Lionel.'

She gave me a look as if between now and that moment in the future anything could happen.

She didn't have a lot of time before her flight. Three hours. I saw her looking around for something.

'You don't have a phone?' she asked. She was back to her

230

inspection, compiling details I was sure would find their way into a letter back to Jean.

'Things are a bit tight right now,' I said. 'So how's Melbourne?'

She ignored that question, pulled her tortoise sunglasses back down and said, 'Come on. Let's go. This place makes me feel nauseous.'

I said it was probably the candlewax smell.

'No, Lionel,' she said. 'It's not that.'

We walked for a while along the empty streets. Meg wasn't in a talkative mood. She walked quickly; it was obvious that Jean had asked her to look me up, that she was here on an errand.

'Sorry about Christmas Day,' I offered.

'So am I,' she said. And a moment later, 'So were Mum and Dad.'

'Were the Wheelers there?'

'What do you think?'

Meg was asserting her moral right as my elder and better. My year away hadn't done anything to close the gap. In Melbourne she had swum ahead into a larger and more sophisticated pool.

It was only after we found a pizza place open down at the waterfront that she dropped the brisk manner and resolved to be friendlier. She began by removing her sunglasses.

'So, tell me about your life,' she said.

I told her about university, the hostel, the food, Brice Johns. All the while shuffling around the real subject.

'Mum said you work in a restaurant?'

'Yep.'

'Is it open?'

'No.'

'Apparently you're quite a dancer these days?'

'I wouldn't say that . . .'

'Dad did, and Mum.'

She took a bite of pizza, her eyes never leaving.

'Tango, they said.'

'Argentinian tango. There's a difference.' I recited my usual mantra on this subject — one is about how you look whereas Argentinian tango was about 'how you feel . . .'

'And Mum mentioned someone . . .' she looked away, pretending that the name escaped her.

'Rosa,' I said.

My sister smiled, her mouth full of pizza now.

'Mum said she came to the house. Dad was very impressed.'

'She runs the restaurant.'

'And you dance with her?'

'Sometimes we do.'

'Do you love her?'

'That's ridiculous. Crazy. I dance with her. She's my employer. She's married, Meg. She's 36-years old.' I was half out of my chair with embarrassment.

'Anyway,' she said. 'I want to talk about Peter.'

She was very worried about him. She hadn't been home for eighteen months so the changes that I had seen take place more gradually were much more pronounced for Meg. She couldn't believe how much our parents had aged. But Peter especially. He was virtually lame. No one had written to warn her of this.

She said, 'I spoke with the doctor. He told me Dad should have had that hip operation in December, Lionel.'

Her eyes flashed up at me.

'He got in a contractor, I hear.'

She gently but firmly corrected that view.

She said, 'The Wheelers are not contractors. They are friends. And while I think of it, Chrissie asked after you.'

She saw me pull a face.

'What? What's that for? She's a lovely girl.'

She looked at her wristwatch and came to the point of what she really meant to say.

'Look,' she said. 'Mum and Dad need you, Lionel. When Dad goes in to hospital next month . . . I can't do anything from Melbourne and it will be over in time for you to get back here. You won't miss the start of the semester.'

'I've already told them I'll be back in time. They know that.'

She didn't answer immediately. She glanced down at her orange juice.

'Mum is worried that you won't be . . .'

'Why wouldn't I?'

She looked back at me quickly and away.

I said. 'Of course I'll be back. I told her. Have you seen that stupid Esperanto she does?'

'She doesn't think it's stupid.'

'Well it is. Totally mindless. Dumb. Stupid shit.'

I was still angry after Meg left for the airport in a taxi. I was glad she was gone because the pool had reopened and I had a feeling Rosa might surprise me there.

233

I changed into my togs but I didn't swim straight away. In the shaded area of the bleachers I sat brooding and thinking about my father's operation. But that was only part of it. I was also dwelling on something that I hadn't shared with Meg. But she had known as well as I did that in my heart of hearts, once I was drawn back to the farm there would be no leaving it again. Meg could board an aeroplane and fly off to Melbourne. I didn't have that option. All I had was a little bit of time left.

The pool superintendent always had a word for me. 'So, how are we today?' or, more puzzlingly, he'd ask 'What do you know?' Squat, dumpy, Matty Diggs got around in sunglasses and shorts that were obscenely small. He never took his eyes off the pool; even when he caught up for a chat his eyes were on the water. He was like a man who can't let his wife wander out of his sight. Diggs of course had many wives.

He joined me now, chewing and talking out the side of his mouth.

'I seen you waiting for someone?'

Well of course even though he had seen me an endless number of times with Rosa I still felt bound to describe her. Diggs nodded, and at a pause in the conversation I added, 'She's from Argentina.'

'You know some interesting people,' he said and stretched out his leg to shift his crotch.

Over the course of the week, at different times he shuffled over to ask me, 'What's doing?'

'Nothing much.'

He nodded like that was pretty well what he expected. He looked at his wristwatch.

'Another no show, huh?'

I shrugged. We both looked up the pool to the turnstile. He looked at his watch again.

'I'd give her another half hour. I hear there's some traffic piled up from the Shore lane off the bridge. So, what can I tell you? Frère Jacques.'

Frère Jacques. Didn't he mean *que sera sera*?

The next day he sided up with the usual 'What do you know?'

'Not much.'

'*Frère Jacques*,' he said.

I didn't want to embarrass the pool superintendent but this time I said to him, 'Actually, the expression is *que sera sera*.'

He turned his sunglasses on me. His jaws stopped rotating.

'You're shitting me?'

'I'm not shitting you.'

'So what's *Frère Jacques*?'

'Brother Jack.'

His jaws started swiftly rotating.

'Brother Jack, you say. Well that doesn't make any sense, does it?'

'Not really,' I said. But I wanted to be more encouraging than that so I added, 'Well, it depends on context. There could be a place or a moment when you say *Frère Jacques*.'

He nodded impatiently.

'Right. Right. Anyway, moving along, how did a young guy like you get shacked up with Mrs Argentina?'

'I'm not shacked up with anybody.'

Diggs stopped chewing. His smile seemed to dangle in mid-air.

'Right', he said. 'That's cool.'

One afternoon Diggs let it be known that he was looking to hire a pool attendant. Actually someone even more junior. An *assistant* pool attendant.

'That sort of thing interest you?'

'Sure,' I said. 'I'm interested.'

'You got a life-saving certificate?'

'No.'

'You have to have a life-saving certificate before I can hire you.'

He went off and got me an instruction booklet. He explained the procedure. At the end of a written examination and 'practical' Diggs would sign the certificate and hire me. It sounded easy enough.

'Have you got someone to practise on? You need someone to practise on for the practical,' he said.

No one came to mind. Diggs thought for a moment.

'What about Argentina?'

'Maybe.'

Diggs was in more of a hurry than that. 'When the kids come back from holiday it's mayhem in here. I can't do it all on my own. You know what I mean? *Que sera*,' he said, and shuffled back to his office.

So far only my sister had shown up to the flat. Where was Rosa? She knew where I lived. She knew I must be sitting here twiddling my thumbs or at the pool. It didn't make sense. I was desperate to see her, if only for a moment. A glimpse would do. Then I started to think, what if something has happened? Something that I don't know about? For all I knew she might be consumed with the same thought, where is Lionel?

This fresh concern was more honourable that mere longing. It gave me an excuse to take the bus past Rosa's house.

The first time there was no movement in the windows. No sign of life. A small kid on a tricycle looked up at the pale longing face in the row of bus windows. The bus picked up speed and the colours of the houses began to run.

I wondered if she had gone on holiday. I got quite worked up thinking that if she had, why hadn't she bothered to tell me?

The next morning I struck gold.

It's amazing all the information that a single glance can gather. Ivan's van parked in the drive. The panting faces of two dogs misting up the side window. Then, as the bus slows and the driver searches for the gear, the front door to Rosa's opens and out she steps in a white bathrobe. She stands aside for Ivan, resplendent in his dog grooming uniform. A blue cotton shirt. Blue cotton trousers. The bus finds its gear and we lurch away from Rosa's peck on Ivan's cheek and some-thing from Ivan that appears to make her laugh. The final view is of her raising a hand to her mouth, a playful shove from Rosa and Ivan dropping down the steps with a self-satisfied smile.

I sat back and looked up the aisle, thinking about what I had seen. That laugh of Rosa's — it was more jousting than anything I was used to. Usually, at least around me, whenever she laughed it was always a controlled response as if the thought processes had to click through the gears of deciding — yes, now I will laugh. With Ivan it had been more spontaneous, more trusting. More intimate?

That night I walked over to Rosa's and stood across the street watching their shadows come and go in the window of the front room.

I stayed out there in the dark until the living room light switched off and the one in the bedroom switched on. I might have crossed the road at that point but one of Ivan's dogs started barking at the side of the house.

The next time I saw them it was by accident. They were walking hand in hand in the gardens near the pool. They walked in that way that lovers do. A slow amble, their hands swinging between them. Their shoulders touched. Ivan raised his wife's hand to his lips. Rosa smiled. I noticed the soft glow of her face. The demure slope of her shoulders. We had never held hands like that. There was that time on the beach on the way to the cave when she had stumbled and reached for my hand; but that didn't count. I'd taken hold of it and released it soon afterwards.

Ivan bought ice-creams for them both and they dawdled along in no hurry. Once they stopped so Rosa could have a lick of Ivan's ice-cream. Some must have dribbled because Ivan caught it on his fingertip and licked it off. They stopped at a kids' playground. And as she pointed to something Ivan shuffled closer. I don't know what held their interest for so long. There was just a bunch of kids doing what kids do in playgrounds. When I looked back Rosa had laid her head on Ivan's shoulder.

They moved on across the grass for a bench under a tree. I saw Ivan remove his jacket and spread it over the bench for Rosa to sit down. She rewarded him with a kiss.

For some time I watched from a circle of trees. Rosa laid her head in Ivan's lap. And Ivan spread his arms along the back rest, looking like the man who has everything. At a certain point, he held up his wristwatch and Rosa sat up. She stood and waited while Ivan shook out his jacket. Then he took Rosa's arm and guided her from the park across the road to a small grey house. They entered the gate and wandered up the path. I waited until they had gone inside then jogged across the road. There was a brass plaque on the gate with the name of a doctor. I looked back at the windows once and ran on.

The next day Rosa is getting into her car when she looks up and sees me in the window. There was no doubt about it. She definitely saw me. And it was like we were viewing one another from two separate worlds for which there was no overlap or intermediary space. The bus and driveway flew by one another, and I was left with the view of her snatching off her sunglasses so as to see better, and then smiling. With that one glance she'd found me out. Though that isn't what ended my trips past her house. I'm sure I wouldn't have been able to help myself. I would have found an excuse to risk more humiliation but for a scratchy throat and runny nose developing into a full blown flu.

For the next two days I listened to the drunk neighbours partying across the street. I saw a skyrocket fly up past my window. I heard the chairs down in the street. This would have been the time for Rosa to arrive at my door and take over. This is what Schmidt had done; he would let himself in to Louise's apartment with 'his' key. After removing his jacket he would take a mop to the tiled floors and open the windows for fresh air and the cheerful noise off the street. Then he'd make Louise a lemon drink and sit by her bed and read to her. For the first time I thought about all the occasions he wouldn't have made it, all those times his imagination must have run bare and he was unable to find an excuse to sneak off to Almagro, and I saw the cost of all that: Louise, ever lonelier, sinking deeper and deeper into exile.

On the day the restaurant was due to reopen, in the early hours of the morning the fever broke. Sweat rolled off me. The sheets stuck to my legs and feet. As the fogginess lifted it was replaced by a scene of horrible clarity. I saw my father struggling on to his farm bike; I saw the gritted teeth of his effort and wave after wave of guilt convulsed me.

Late that afternoon, cars stacked with surfboards blasted by for the beach. Small kids ran in and out of lawn sprinklers. I walked in a deathly sweat all the way to La Chacra.

Only two waitresses were on duty. Kay and the others were still on holiday. We were down to a skeleton staff; we were expecting a quiet time to begin with. Angelo was setting up in the carvery. He sang out to me as I came in through the door.

'It's the dancing man. You're back!'

He sounded surprised. Why wouldn't I be back? I wondered if Rosa had said something.

'And Angelo, I see you're back?'

'Si. For now, Angelo is back.'

He sounded a touch regretful. I couldn't imagine Angelo anywhere else. Nor could I imagine La Chacra without him. He bunched a towel in his hand and lifted a pot of simmering pasta off the stove.

'So, what can I make for you? The blue cheese and walnut sauce?'

'Great,' I said. I hadn't eaten in days. I hadn't tasted Angelo's food since Christmas Eve.

Angelo gave a heavy sigh. 'I thought so. The year changes, but nothing else.'

It was a slow night. The waitresses drifted out to the kitchen and then out to the loading bay to smoke. Once Angelo came back to fetch one of the waitresses. 'The pesto for table twelve,' he said without any urgency, then he stayed out there himself for a cigarette. I didn't need to be told that Rosa hadn't come in.

The next night she is in and there's no talk of the bus. She seems as happy to see me as I am to see her. The night can't end quickly enough.

After everyone has gone we turn up the music. We dance slowly — it's been such a long time. We dance the usual steps, the ones that are second nature to me now, but it is different. It is different because of what has happened and for the way that everything is left unsaid. As I think that, I realise my error. It *is* said. It is said by the way we dance.

Troilo's 'Danzarín' ends with his signature rush — the sort of thing that makes petals stand on end. Our faces are an inch apart, Rosa's eyes sparkling with mischief and pleasure. I want to kiss her. She knows that, of course. She removes her hand from my shoulder and distances herself with a backward step.

'Now,' she says, 'you're discovering at last what it is to dance.'

This is the night we have special favours to ask of each other. She goes first. She wants me to help Ivan with his dog grooming. She's quick to overrule any objection. 'Well you did say I forget how many times you need to make more money . . .' The thing is, she says, Ivan suffers from psoriasis. Whenever his skin complaint flares up he has to pull back from actual dog washing. 'So he needs someone to help him. I told him you might do it.'

I'm not sure I want to be that close to Ivan.

'Can I think about it?'

'Actually, I told him you would do it. But if that is unreasonable. . .'

'No. No.'

'Good. Then it is settled. I believe you also have something to ask of me . . .'

'Life-saving,' I start to say.

I tell her about Diggs's offer and explain the need to practise the 'kiss of life' on someone.

'The kiss of life.' She repeats it after me. She likes that.

– 32 –

So now I'm washing dishes at night and dogs during the day. There are different combs for different dogs depending on whether it's a shorthaired dog or one of those long-haired mutts with two date eyes. I even brush their teeth. Ivan has a special toothbrush and special chicken-flavoured dog toothpaste. All the dogs become skittish around water – their tails droop. But they love having their teeth brushed. Their eyes look at you when you do this, and it's like they're thinking, isn't this interesting, and, thank you, thank you.

Rosa had made the arrangements. The first morning I waited nervously for Ivan to show outside the restaurant. Lines of early morning traffic streamed by. Then the van I'd seen in Rosa's drive swung out of a centre lane. I stepped away from the doors of La Chacra and the van met me at the curb. Ivan leant across to open the door and as I got in he said, 'Lionel, is it?' With the engine running we shook hands. 'Give the door a decent slam. That's it.' After I closed the door the air was suddenly close with dog breath and panting. I turned to find two big animals with black gums and drooling pink tongues.

'That's Jazz and that's Veronica.' And to the dogs he said, 'This is Lionel.'

That was pretty much it until we arrived at his dog grooming base. Thereafter it was all instruction. Do this . . . make sure you use this . . . 'And watch the basenji. They're a temperamental breed. A basenji will read you like a book. They know your attitude. Approach them with respect. Treat thy neighbour, etcetera. Know what I mean, Lionel?'

'Yes, sir.'

'Ivan will do.'

After my second day he asked me if I had togs. 'Better bring them along tomorrow.' There was no further explanation. The next day I was just getting into the swing of clipping dog toenails, combing their hanks, and even massaging their bony skulls, that marrowy bit between their eyes, and their arthritic hindquarters when Ivan asked me to get in the bath with Giselle, a temperamental poodle in for a 'hydrotherapeutic treatment'. Suddenly I had an insight into the conversation that Rosa must have had with Ivan. 'Yes, of course he can swim. He loves swimming. He spends every afternoon at the pool.'

I was used to dogs. But the dogs I knew were working dogs, farm dogs. I'd spent most of my life around dogs. The dogs that came through Ivan's door were 'kept dogs'. They seemed to know they were different. We'd pick them up from different neighbourhoods and courier them back to the grooming place. Along the way the dogs to be groomed would look out the van windows at the dogs in the street. A certain sniffiness was transmitted. Lots of ear twitching and gaping from the street dogs. And stony Winston Churchill gazing from the groomed dogs.

That's pretty much how Ivan and I acted around each other. Me with the constant fear that I would say something that would give me away; something of my inner life would bubble to the surface, or worse, Ivan would recognise some private truth to do with his wife known only to himself. It would spring from me, written all over my face.

After my first day with Ivan, Rosa came back to the kitchen to ask how it had gone.

I thought it had gone well.

'So you are learning about dogs,' she said drolly.

'I already know about dogs. I grew up with them, don't forget.'

'Ah,' she said. 'Jean called. I just remembered. She called, then you came in and Angelo dropped a plate and I forgot. So.'

'What did she want?'

'She was so nice. She tried some Esperanto and I spoke in Spanish and she could understand some of it.'

'Does she want me to call her?'

'She said you would know and just to say that she had called.'

She gave me a querying look.

'Everything is all right, Pasta?'

'As far as I know, everything is all right. You're the one who spoke to her.'

'Well,' she said. 'You know where the phone is. I think it would be nice if you called Jean.'

I switched my attention back to the dishes. I felt uncomfortable discussing my mother with her.

'And so, you and Ivan got on well?'

'No problem. He loves his dogs, doesn't he?'

'Yes,' she said. 'Perhaps he loves his dogs too much.'

I went on to tell her about the dogs I'd met that day. Betsy, a slow patient Labby that had stood with such a melancholic expression that Ivan wondered if she was depressed. I'd washed her twice, the second time with warm water to relax her for a massage. After Betsy there was Trevor, a collie, and Rex, a sausage dog. It was interesting how each dog responded differently: Rex with a toothy pornographic grin as I rubbed down his limbs.

And later, much later that night when we turned up 'Los Argentinos' to dance, she asked me again about Ivan.

I said, 'He doesn't say much, does he?'

'Well Ivan is different. A different kind of man.'

We were on the verge of private information. I waited. She was about to say more when she sniffed, sniffed again, and stepped back from me.

'Oh God, that smell. That disinfectant. I am so used to smelling it on Ivan. Now you two smell the same.'

Her face froze. Goyeneche sang on.

'No,' she said, releasing herself from me. 'You will have to wash it off, Lionel. I cannot dance with that smell . . .'

She led me back to the kitchen where she filled the sink with warm

246

water. She poured in the detergent I washed the dishes with, then she got me to strip off my shirt and began to wash me with a sponge that I used to wipe down the benches. I felt like a dog, with Rosa my groomer. I had to lean over the bench so she could wash my back. She didn't scrub. She washed in a caressing kind of way. Then she dried me, and while she was doing that I felt her mouth hover over my back. Then she turned me and kissed each nipple, drifting her fingers down that line to the top of my jeans. 'What a handsome *compadrito*. Now we can dance.'

Cautiously we felt our way, each step probing an area of uncertainty before committing the rest of us. To a casual onlooker, to Ivan say, pulling up at the window and looking in, we would have seemed very intimate. The tension in me had everything to do with the possibility of Ivan crashing in on this moment.

When I got home I showered, and in the morning I showered again to make sure Ivan would not smell his wife on me.

My days and nights were spent involved with water of one kind of another. January was hot and humid. After five or six hours of splashing around with the dogs I would try to squeeze in a swim at the pool before heading off to the restaurant.

Changes were happening there, small things that passed unnoticed at the time and only really acquired significance much later in the piece. Restaurants are a fickle business. All a restaurant has to offer is a menu and an atmosphere, and these things are as faddish and ephemeral as the season's fashion statement.

Here it is — a Wednesday night and one of the waitresses has been sent home early. I can't recall that ever happening before. Then again I can't recall business being this quiet. And Angelo — that's his voice I can hear joking and flirting with the waitresses out on the landing. That means Rosa can't be about. Sure enough, when I pop out to the door her booth is vacant. A scattering of silent diners are sawing into their steaks. Something is going on that I can't put my finger on. Later, when the dishes come in they arrive in one tidy pile. I feed the machine and wait, and while I'm doing that Angelo trundles back with his meat trays, just the two, plus his carving knives. He's hardly raised a sweat all night.

When I ask him, 'What's going on out there, Angelo? It's as dead a doormat . . .' he shrugs, like he isn't paid to wonder or care.

Then he says mischievously and with a mad glint in his eye, 'Maybe Rosa and Ivan try to make baby?' And he makes a crude little gesture with his fingers. He watches me as he does that, lewd, calculating, and with the knowledge that he's working something into a wound he's just opened. Angelo is not the friend I thought I had. Still I don't want to get on his bad side while he's feeding me.

'Babies. You know?' he says, laughing and shaking his head.

Babies. I don't find it nearly as hilarious as Angelo does. I don't find it funny at all. All the same, it does set me wondering.

The next day, in the van on our way to pick up a basenji, I'm quieter than I normally am; even Ivan notices this and asks if I'm all right.

I tell him I'm ok. A bit tired maybe. A pat answer and the world rolls safely onwards.

'Good,' he says. 'That's good.'

Out at this house in the western suburbs where we've come to pick up a basenji I find myself naturally taking the dog's side. I'm watching the dog and so is Ivan. Ivan is pretending to look elsewhere; the dog is waiting for Ivan to discover him. But Ivan's floating gaze cannot be diverted from the distant hills, the clouds. The basenji sits on his sharp hindquarters, its snout following Ivan's eyes. Its tongue hangs in the angled part of its jaw and there is something playful and knowing about the loll of its tongue like it really wants to say to Ivan, 'You silly fucker.' I don't know how he's going to get this mutt in the van. The booking is for a massage and shampoo and comb. Ivan's eyes will eventually meet with the basenji's. There's no avoiding it. You can see the basenji is thinking the same thing. The basenji's thinking, I can do this. I can sit here for as long as it takes.

While this is going on I'm thinking, it's five weeks now since I've had full-blown sex with Rosa. A lot of nibbling around the edges since. I start thinking about her breasts, the beautiful warm snare of her legs and hair. I'm starting to become aroused when one of the dogs in the van barks. Ivan looks up slightly annoyed, as if that were my fault. The other dogs are cramming the window to see what will happen. You can see that they're all willing anarchy into the head of the basenji. The basenji nods in their direction like he knows the game. Now Ivan starts to whistle softly. He's found a grassblade to inspect. Now my employer is rolling on his side on the lawn and the basenji is coming over to lick his face.

Back in the van with the captured dog and Ivan's face filled with aftermatch glow, he says: 'You let them think they're the centre of atention and you're history. That's your basenji for you, Lionel.' He looks across at me with a drizzly smile, and I think, what I am supposed to draw from this? Is it this? He may not be physically present at the restaurant after hours when Rosa and I dance, alone, but his antennae are up and floating over the city and peering into every sinkhole and crevice. Is this what he means? Or is he really just talking about dogs?

For the second night in a row Rosa has failed to show up at the restaurant. Kay is back on and running the ship. To my mind Kay has always looked part of the furnishings, as though she arrived in the same removal truck that delivered the booths, the red carpet and the stained wood. Tonight she looks younger and fresher. She is tanned from her beach holiday. Her eyes look bigger and brighter. She's put a blonde rinse through her hair. For the first time I can imagine her with a life elsewhere. This is a luxury that I don't have.

Back in the kitchen I'm feeling maudlin. No Rosa means no dancing and no intimacy for the second night running. Again we finish up early, and when Angelo comes back with his trays the sight of me gives him pleasure. He laughs and mutters something in Spanish. I don't understand any of it except one word, 'Romeo'. And as he leaves me to it he gives his crude finger-fucking gesture.

The next day I'm more lucky. On our way to make a pick-up we stop by Rosa and Ivan's house to get some dog ownership papers. As we pull up the drive Ivan says, 'Might as well switch on the jug since we're here.' In the hall, every step I take seems to creak with the whole overlap of my life with Rosa.

Then there comes a *corte*, one of those turnstile moments. It is as we are wandering up the hall when Rosa steps from the bathroom in her bathrobe, her hair swaddled in towels. This is the first time that the three of us have been in the same room.

Rosa ignores Ivan. She says to me, 'Ah, it's my favourite dish-washer.'

She kisses my cheek. Her bathrobe parts and I smell her soapy scent.

'Don't I get one?'

Ivan is standing there in the hall, grinning. Rosa slaps her hands on to her hips while she decides whether Ivan deserves a kiss.

'Have you been good?' she asks.

'I'm always good. You know that.'

The two of them are grinning at each other. Rosa's look is one of kind regard. Ivan's is of the adoring cocker spaniel kind. For half a second it's as if I'm not there. For half a second I think back to Angelo's teasing gesture. So Angelo is there in the hall with us; so is Billy Pohl and Henry Graham, and I have a feeling that I must look like they did, envious, resentful of the chemistry between Schmidt and Louise. It's the same old dance.

'In that case . . .' says Rosa.

Ivan closes his eyes and offers his cheek. But it is a discounted kiss — a kiss on the end of her fingertip which she attaches to him.

In the kitchen she becomes more adventurous. While we are waiting for the jug to boil she says to Ivan, 'I've been helping Lionel with his life-saving.'

I don't think Ivan heard. Thank God. The jug is burbling away and

Ivan's attention is elsewhere. He's turning the pages of his diary for the address of the lovely mild-tempered collie bitch sitting patiently out in the van. Colette was booked in for a long brush, massage and hydrotherapy.

'Where are you? Where are you? Carl. Choisa. Connie. Colette.'

He looks up to find the two of us observing him.

'What?' he asks.

'Life-saving,' says Rosa. 'Lionel is sitting for his certificate.'

Still Ivan is none the wiser. He looks at me, then back at Rosa.

'What certificate?'

'His life-saving. Here, we'll show you.'

Without another word she drops to the kitchen floor and pretends to be the 'drowning person'. One hand is flung dramatically above her head. Her eyes are closed while she waits to be saved.

Ivan looks perplexed and slightly irritated. He's thinking, will this take long? His eyebrows bristle. He checks the time on his watch.

'Lionel, I am drowning.'

I check first with Ivan. 'All right, go ahead,' he says. I drop to my knees and roll Rosa on to her back. I lift her jaw and tilt the head back. Under the circumstances I'm not about to do mouth-to-mouth. So I close Rosa's mouth and seal my mouth over her nose and give four quick breaths.

'Okay,' I announce to Ivan's frowning face. 'Now we watch for the chest to rise.'

That's what we do. The two of us stare at Rosa's ample chest, Ivan with a cup of tea in his hand. In her own good time Rosa's chest begins to rise.

'There,' he says dourly. 'She's alive.'

He glances at his watch again. Immediately we're back on dog watch. There is a 'collect' he wants me to do later. He's double-booked a shampoo with a toe-clipping and massage.

'Freddy's the spaniel's name. Now be gentle with him. In fact, if I were you, I'd carry him out to the van. The old woman will be watching to see how you interact . . .'

Then the voice from the floor speaks up.

'See, he does not care if I drown or survive. All he cares about is his dogs. His schnauzers. Corgis. Foxies. Toe-clippings and dog massage.'

Back in the van Ivan is more talkative than usual, more interested in me. He's interested to know how long I have been life-saving, how my interest came about, that sort of thing.

Rosa is in the restaurant that night. It's busier than the previous three or four nights, but still nothing to get carried away with. But with Rosa back at the tiller there is a keenness amongst the waitresses. Tonight they are looking for things to do without first being asked. The door between the front and back of the kitchen swings back and forth all night long. For the first time in a while the tape deck is switched on; later, I smile to myself as I hear Gardel turned up. I rush through the last of the dishes and pans, wipe down the benches, dump my apron and present myself at the front of the restaurant.

There are no stragglers. No hangers-on among the waitresses, thank God. The chairs have already been put upside down on the tables. So the space is cleared and ready for dancing. The compilation of steak-eating standards 'La Cumparsita', 'El Choclo' and 'Felicia' have been turned up. Only this time, rather than dance, Rosa says she wants to be 'rescued'.

'This morning you didn't do such a good job of saving me. I want the kiss of life this time,' she says.

She doesn't wait for an answer. Already she is crouching down to place herself on her back. I wait until she has arranged things. Then I get down on my knees and begin to clear her air passages. I turn her head this way and that. I lay her exhausted limbs at her side. Now I pinch her nose and she shakes her head. 'Not the nose one, Lionel. The kiss of life. Yes? Good. Then let us proceed.

And this is what Ivan sees. My mouth placed over his wife's mouth.

This is what he says: 'Lionel?'

His voice isn't raised. There's no anger, let alone rage. Just a polite inquiry. *Lionel.* I look up. And there he is — in the doorway. His hands which usually live in his trouser pockets hang at his sides. They look as if they want to grab hold of something. We must have missed him during the orchestral section of 'La Cumparsita'. There's a look of distress on his face. But a little perplexity is hanging in there as well, as if to say, if I'm quick about it he might be open to an explanation.

But I'm not quick. I'm far from quick. I've never been in a situation like this before. I'm in deep over my head. And it's left to Rosa to talk our way out of this.

'He is saving my life,' she says matter-of-factly. There's not a single trace of fear or apology. It's as if she is snappish and irritated with Ivan for interrupting this critical moment in her resuscitation.

Ivan hasn't taken his eyes off me.

'Is that what you're doing, Lionel? Life-saving? Is that what I'm seeing here?'

'Sure.'

And I don't feel like I'm lying when I say this.

Diggs is testing me for my certificate in a day's time. I explain this to Ivan, and go on a bit about the various methods: mouth-to-nose, mouth-to-mouth.

As Rosa picks herself up from the floor Ivan's interest switches to her.

'There,' she says, and she takes a deep thank-God-I've-made-it-back-to-the-beach breath. Absurdly, all three of us look in the vague direction of the sea. We listen to Rosa's improbable account: 'I was swimming and suddenly this large breaker crashed down on me and pulled me under. I couldn't breathe. I thought I would drown. Then I felt the strong arms of my faithful dishwasher around me.'

She smiled gratefully.

'Thank you, Lionel.'

She looked unflinchingly back at Ivan.

'If you were a husband who loved his wife you would thank Lionel for his heroics.'

By now Ivan is looking very fidgety. His eyes are twitching dangerously. You can see him struggling with what to believe, as opposed to what he has to believe.

He says to me, 'I guess I'll be seeing you, Lionel.' And as he says this his eyes stay fixed on me for an unnatural length of time.

'Sure. Tomorrow,' I answer.

To Rosa he gives a curt nod. They haven't finished discussing this by any stretch of the imagination.

'I'll see you at home,' he says.

We watch him leave. Wait until his shadow passes by the restaurant front and we hear the van start up. About now I remember to breathe again. I feel terrible. Typically, Rosa is ready to move on to the next thing. She comes towards me with her figurehead smile. It's a case of where were we . . . oh yes. 'Now we can dance,' she says.

The next day when I showed up at Ivan's plant his van wasn't there and the door was locked. An envelope marked for my attention was pinned to the door. Inside it was a cheque for the money Ivan owed me, and a note thanking me for my help but saying he felt he could manage on his own.

– 33 –

I WAS HOLDING ON TO AN EXTRA FEW DAYS. A FEW MORE DAYS TO ENJOY Rosa if I could. Come the end of the month I'd be back home, on the farm. Between now and that moment I was determined to extract as much as I could from the little time left to us.

Diggs didn't need me at the pool until 11.30 am. So until then I was free to do whatever I wanted. I asked Rosa if she would come to my flat. It was perfectly safe; Ivan would be working with the dogs. She was hesitant, her explanation uncharacteristically vague.

'It's not so easy, Lionel.'

'You can drive over at nine. What's so hard about that?'

'Well as you know, for one thing I am asleep. And besides . . .'

'Besides what?'

257

'And besides now you're hectoring me.'

She didn't know of my plan to leave at the end of the month. She didn't know of the abyss staring back at me. I was planning to tell her soon. But that, like the difficulty of leaving on a particular day, kept shifting ground.

'You could come to the pool,' I said. 'You never come to the pool. I miss our time there and the stories.'

It didn't strike me as a big thing to ask but Rosa appeared to turn it around and look at it from all angles.

'Yes,' she said. 'This once I will come.'

The weight she gave the word 'once' passed me by at the time.

After weeks of bathing with filthy dogs the sparkling water of the Stanley Hope Pool was dazzling, the last of January's heat lifting the reek of chlorine from the damp patches. The jostling bodies. The girls flirting under my zinc nose. I don't know how it started but somehow my name had got around the pool. *Hi Lionel! Over here. Hey, Lionel!*

During the lunch hour I had to be my on mettle. The lane swimmers, women mostly from offices downtown, hated getting splashed. If anyone banged into them they stopped swimming, and trod water while they raised their goggles to glare at me or Diggs, as if it were our fault. The older women in their tight one-piece bathing suits, bathing caps and goggles, treated the water like work, ploughing up and down the lanes. Afterwards they dragged their joyless bodies up the steps, their faces and heavy thighs covered in red splotches of exertion. By comparison Rosa got in and out of the water, almost amphibiously. She swam effortlessly, too, the water neatly parting for her, whereas the other women appeared to push a wall of water ahead of themselves.

The pool was a different constituency from the one at La Chacra — they were kids a year or two younger than myself. I'd forgotten that world and its close, exploratory, furtive ways. A boy and girl getting off on each other's charge as they lay together on the hot tiles, their sides just touching.

I saw all these things while I waited for Rosa to show up. Contrary to her word, day after day passed where she failed to show.

At the restaurant I'd ask her what happened. Why didn't she come? These conversations were always rushed since she seemed to be juggling things more and more, the restaurant and some undisclosed area of her life outside. I noticed her on the phone a lot more, smiling into the receiver. She often went early and left Kay or Angelo to lock up.

Or else Ivan was there these days to pick her up.

So we weren't even dancing any more.

When I peppered her with questions she looked sorry and regretful. She didn't know what to say to me. Finally, one night as I was badgering her, she stopped me to say she had some news.

'Yes?'

What possible news could be more important than her reason for not coming to the pool?

'Not now. Not here,' she said, glancing around the kitchen.

'But you will tell me?'

'Yes.'

'When?'

'Tomorrow. Tomorrow I will come to the pool.'

'So tomorrow you will definitely come? You promise?'

'This I said already. Now you are nagging me,' she said.

She didn't say at what time. I decided it would be early afternoon. That would give her time to wake up, shower, knock back her orange juice and black coffee, and still have time before she needed to think about the restaurant. Not that she seemed to give it much thought these days. A drunk in the night had thrown a beer bottle and shattered the glass in a corner of the large front window. That was a week ago. Instead of getting it replaced, she'd asked me to help Angelo tape some cardboard over the web of broken glass.

Around one o'clock I started getting restless. Diggs noticed me casting my eyes in the direction of the turnstile so he started checking his watch from time to time, responding to my anxiety with a shrug of his shoulders, a tug at his crotch.

One o'clock passed. Then two o'clock. She wasn't coming. I'd already decided. The next time I looked up it was four o'clock. I found myself pulling up kids for things I would usually let pass. I was a black cloud circling the pool.

Then, just before closing time, without any expectation, I happened to look up the end of the pool and there she was. Usually she strode through the turnstile twirling her magisterial hands ahead of her. But this wasn't the Rosa who had shown up. This Rosa was far less confident of herself. As she came closer I saw all that uncertainty that accompanies bad news. For that is what I'd decided I was about to hear.

The last swimmer was getting out. A few more picked up their towels and made towards the changing rooms.

'I'm late. I'm sorry,' she said.

She snuck a quick look back up the pool in the direction of Diggs's office.

'I'll be quick. I'll be in and out before you know it.'

'Be my guest,' I said.

'Thank you.'

It was a strangely formal exchange. Diggs came out of the Men's with a hose in his hand. The sight of Rosa took him by surprise. As she walked by him they exchanged a nod; then Diggs turned and followed her with his eyes. Then he sought me out with a what-the-hell-do-you-think-you're-doing look. He tapped his watch. I called across the pool that everything was all right — 'I'll lock up' — and that just caused him to look heavenwards. He'd never let me lock up before. Today wasn't going to be any different.

There was a light splash and we both looked down at the dark shadow moving underwater. There was something wilful and attractively casual about her decision to forego her usual bathing cap. She broke the surface, her eyelids beautifully composed, lips pursed, more pink than red. Then everything opened in her face at once. She found me on the side of the pool and smiled. Diggs rolled his eyes and dragged his hose up to the toddlers' shed at the top of the pool.

For the rest of Rosa's swim I picked up articles of clothing left behind. A sodden towel. A child's white singlet. By the time I came out of the changing rooms I was relieved to see that she was true to her word. It was a short swim and she was already out of the pool. That meant I could start the chlorine. The pump room was by the entrance to the Women's, and that's where I was when I heard Rosa call out — 'Lionel? Lionel? Is that you?' It was the voice of someone caught up a tree and slightly embarrassed to be calling for help.

I looked around for Diggs. His office window was ablaze with the late-afternoon sun. As I stepped inside the entrance of the Women's I was thinking, this is probably a sackable offence. I didn't know how I would explain it to Diggs. A woman's cry for help. That cat-up-a-tree thought. I could hear the shower running, so I called quietly ahead — just in case someone unaccounted for was still in the shed, and Rosa answered back: 'Lionel, thank goodness. I thought I had been deserted. Be a sweet and get my towel. It's with my bag. I left it on the steps.'

I tried to be casual about it and pick up Rosa's things as I would the belongings of anyone else. This time, as I slipped back inside the Women's, Rosa must have seen my shadow on the wall and noted its hesitancy, because she called out: 'Come on, Lionel. There's nothing to be shy about.'

As I came around the corner I was surprised by the long view of Rosa dripping wet under the showerhead. She stood tall, her right shoulder pointing away from me, her right hand cupping her left breast. She was beautiful.

She smiled back at me. 'My lifesaver,' she said.

As I approached she dropped her hand away from her breast and presented all of herself. She raised her arms and it was clear to me what she wanted. She wanted me to dry her — here and there. But as I moved towards her she stepped back into the shower jet.

'If I let you touch me, Lionel, it must be for the last time.'

Touch. Last. These are the words I hear over the shower.

Then she says: 'I am pregnant. I am going to have Ivan's baby.'

'Pregnant?'

She nods, her wet hair sticking to the side of her face. I have never seen her so happy.

I kneel then so she can't see me. I don't want her to see how upset I am. I don't know where these damn tears sprung from.

I start with her legs, not dwelling on but not ignoring either the rich tangle of hair. I feel her hand touch my face. She brings me higher but not so high; she invites me to drift and drift and she purrs at the place my mouth goes. The only sound we hear is the shower water and the gurgling of that water going down the drain.

– 34 –

Each of us carries our fatal flaw within. Schmidt, who was so used to doorways and glancing views — on the bus bound for Chacarita — the flower of broom clipping his eye and launching him out of his seat. Blinding him to the traffic and all consideration of safety.

Louise would have acquired some Spanish. She must have. The words that come first are always those ones which are self-explanatory. *Tipa blanco* are those trees with the black and stricken branches which in spring sprinkle white-tipped flowers over the city pavements. *Tipa blanco*. The same flowers used to stick to the heels of Louise's shoes.

The simplest vocabulary might have saved her life. On the day the lifts in her apartment building broke down she might have taken greater care had she read the sign at the top of the landing warning tenants of the slippery stairs. A distraught caretaker, cap in hand, later told the authorities that he had arranged for signs to be placed on every landing. Louise took no heed. In too much of a hurry she had stepped carelessly, the heel of her dancing shoe slipping on the edge of the step. She landed on her tailbone, her head bouncing with fatal impact against the concrete.

At a *milonga* in Almagro, Paul Schmidt sat waiting, and waiting.

Death ends all things and La Chacra was no exception.

It started with Angelo's departure. Rosa pleaded with him to stay but after Angelo resisted all attempts at flattery and, finally, bribes, Rosa washed her hands of him. With breathtaking dexterity she let it be known that Angelo wasn't such a great chef anyhow. She'd find another, this time a better chef. Angelo knew only the one thing; had just the one trick up his sleeve. La Chacra needed to develop a more adventurous menu.

A succession of chefs followed, the menu changing as many times until Ernie Buckler arrived to turn the steaks on the grill. Ernie had worked on the ferries and in canteens that fed up to two hundred at one sitting. With Ernie arrived a new clientele; most of them seemed to know 'Ernie boy'. They shook their heads at the offer of the wine list, asked for beer, and finished with endless cups of tea.

The decline had begun before Angelo's departure but after he left a more general haemorrhaging took place. Once upon a time you'd have needed a booking on a Friday or Saturday night. Now you could walk in the door and pick a table.

Kay left for a new restaurant in town and a new position. *Maitre d'*.

Rosa didn't appreciate how important Kay was until she left. By then it was too late. There followed a dizzy period where the restaurant had to weather a complete turnover of waitresses.

There was no more hiding the carpet stains, the stiffness of its fibre; no amount of disinfectant could overcome the stale aroma.

The decline was just as self-evident at the back of the kitchen. The walk-in fridge was a shrine to better times when Angelo's famous *créme caramel* sat in floor-to-ceiling trays. Ernie's deserts didn't require the same amount of preparation. The pile of dishes failed to mount to much. Quite often, and to my pleasant surprise, he cleaned his own pans.

Rosa looked tired. She looked older. Her thirty-seventh birthday came and went. She had kept the day a secret. That night she cited some vague business that would take her away from the restaurant for a few hours. I learnt later that she and Ivan had gone off to a flashier restaurant down at the waterfront.

The next night, it was near the end of my shift, Rosa visited me out in the kitchen. I handed her a poem I'd written that day. The words are lost to memory — fortunately. I seem to recall that I made something of her name — Rosa/Rose. But she read it generously, her eyes burning into the sheet of paper. She was halfway through it when I had the thought that maybe it wasn't the right thing to have done, and that in fact the poem wasn't much good. She reached the end and looked up. 'So you are now a poet and a historian — as well as a dancer?' She smiled up at me, at my youthfulness; and as if she had just caught a glimpse of all the surprises still to be sprung in me, she said, 'Come here.' I bent down to present my cheek and receive my award. 'No,

Lionel. Here.' She turned my head so she could kiss me properly on the lips. She placed her hand against my jaw, to hold the kiss. To make it linger. Now I know it as the kiss which signals farewell; where one retains the contact in order to better remember. When we parted she said, 'Lionel, I have some news for you.' She'd just come off the phone from speaking with Jean.

My father had gone to help an old ewe that had trapped its head in the fenceline. Peter left his farm bike and managed to roll himself down the slope to where the ewe was trapped in the wire. He freed the sheep and lying on his side watched it wander away. He managed to raise himself to his elbows and drag himself a few metres before he became stuck. His legs were a dead weight. He couldn't move another inch. He tried and tried; and at some point it must have been easier to just lie there and wait.

Around dusk my mother had begun to worry. With the last light about to disappear over the hilltops she went out to look for him. She didn't get far. Soon it was dark, and she hurried back to call up the Wheelers. They came over immediately. Well into the night they fanned out over the tracks with their torches. Chrissie found him around 5 am. My father had suffered a heart attack. He was already dead.

– 35 –

THE HILLS AND SKY WERE WAITING FOR ME. LOOK WHAT YOU'VE DONE.
Look what you did. It's all your fault, you realise that, don't you? That's
what they seemed to be saying, and as I wound down the hill road to
the farmhouse I felt like I was descending a hole with no way out, no
way back.

My mother, the one person entitled to lay blame at my feet,
wrapped her arms around me and held her frail body against me. Harry
Wheeler was next in line. My father's oldest friend and neighbour laid
his hand on my shoulder and with a few chosen words I felt my guilt
lift and forgiveness settle in its place. Last in line, so to speak, was the
doctor. He caught up with me on the phone. 'That you, Lionel? Listen,
it's not a bad way to go,' he told me. 'Once you pass fifty a finger can

268

reach out and touch your shoulder and over you go. That's the thing about heart attacks. There doesn't have to be any prior symptons. It's not like a sniffle leading up to a cold. There's no warning. It picks its moment. I've arrived on the scene to a man crumpled on the floor still holding his shaver, slumped at the wheel of his truck, in the bath, halfway through a slice of toast, holding his fishing rod . . .'

I walked outside and breathed the farm air and stared up at the hills and sky. The sky kept moving overhead as it had always done. I looked up the hill and saw a motorcycle sketch a shadow against the hillside above the road. Chrissie was one more element waiting to fit around me.

It was Chrissie's hand I felt at my shoulder during Peter's funeral. And it was her shadow that slipped alongside mine almost unnoticed at first in the weeks and months after.

I don't recall a more brutal winter. Condensation on the farmhouse windows turned to ice in the night. Ice covered the old wheel tracks of my father's farm bike and cracked underfoot as slowly and inexorably I found myself walking into his life. Snow blanketed the tops. The air had only to make a slight shift to cut through to the bone. June, July, August, and for a week in late September, I dug tracks through the snow for the marooned merino flock to follow me down to the lower slopes. I had help, and I'd hear Chrissie whistling and shouting at her eye dog. She wasn't so shy on the tops. We'd meet back at the farmhouse; circling back by different routes to Jean's soup tureen bubbling on the stove top. When we saw only two places set at the table Jean would give an apologetic smile. She wasn't hungry. Or she had already eaten. There was never time to argue the point. She was already half out the door.

One hot December day I watched Chrissie track back to the ute from the post office. We'd been on a week-long muster and we were both feeling as fit as buck rabbits. Chrissie's face was tanned, healthy looking, healthier than anyone else's in town. Through her denim jeans I could sense her strong lean thighs. The word 'coltish' comes to mind. I may have read that somewhere. But whoever came up with that word must have caught a glimpse of Chrissie that day. I saw the way she turned heads; and one old face from school went out of his way to stop her in the street. He was delighted to see her. When I saw how pleased she looked in return I made a snap decision.

By the time she got back in the ute I was ready to ask her to marry me. I didn't at that precise moment. The actual asking bit came later.

It was a two-hour drive back to the farm. Once she looked across to ask if anything was the matter. I must have been feeling pleased with myself because I couldn't stop grinning.

Back at the farmhouse she picked up her motorcycle helmet to ride back to the Wheelers. She kept turning the helmet in her hands. She was reluctant to leave. I couldn't think what to say that would delay her; some small talk, farm matters which we gave too grave a consideration until, at last — fortunately — Jean came to the rescue.

'I've got a lasagne coming out of the oven in forty minutes. I've made far too much.'

She looked at Chrissie when she said that; Chrissie briefly looked at me.

And because my mother rightly divined that something else was required, she said, 'There's some cold beer in the fridge. Why don't you two go out to the porch and I'll bring a tray out to you.'

Chrissie smiled down at the helmet in her hands. She didn't know what to do with it until I took it from her.

After dinner Jean slipped away to her bedroom. I put on 'Danzarin'.

Chrissie was halfway through picking up her beer glass when she put it down again. I held out my arms to her.

'Here,' I said. 'I'm going to teach you to dance.'